Boonville

Boonville

Boonville Trilogy (Book 1)

Ryan J. Pelton

This is a work of fiction. Names, characters, places, and incidents either are the products of the author's imagination or are used fictitiously. Any resemblance to actual persons, living or dead, businesses, companies, events, or locales is entirely coincidental.

Edited by Danielle Larkin

Published by *Attention Books*

attentionbooks.com

ISBN (Print): 978-1-949420-14-2

Prologue

The town of Boonville sits near the rushing waters of the Missouri River. A small and quaint town a hundred miles from Kansas City. A city with deep roots spanning thousands of years from Native Americans to Daniel Boone to Lewis and Clark and to another menace working in the shadows.

Don't let the rich history of this small town along the river seduce you into thinking all is well. Something is rumbling under the picturesque tree-lined streets and shops on Main Street and vast farmland on the outskirts of town. Don't let the plastic smiles seduce you into an innocence; well, that doesn't exist.

Blood is on their hands, and looks can be deceiving.

Chapter One

Charlie slammed the back door of the First Baptist Church of Kansas City fifteen-passenger van. He walked around the perimeter of the vehicle and checked the tire pressure, oil, and seat belts. The things he learned to test for his Class B license. Charlie took a deep breath, still baffled Dad trusted twelve souls into his hands.

Charlie Tanner wasn't much older than the high school group of kids from the First Baptist Church. He'd just graduated high school and was navigating choices between college and work. Becoming an assistant pastor in training was not high on the priority list, but Dad was persuasive. The idea of taking useless general education classes at a local college, with no clear path of a career, seemed like a waste of time and money.

The van fired up, and the kids waved to their families standing in the church parking lot. Charlie gripped the wheel and waved along with the kids. *Why in the world would these parents entrust the safety of their children into my hands? I just got my license two years ago. But here we are.*

Charlie made a pathetic speech about respect and not

being too loud and then hopped on highway seventy while plugging coordinates into his phone. The estimated arrival time just before lunch. A ninety-mile trek to Boonville, Missouri, where Camp Hickory Hill is located.

Boonville is a picturesque town on the Missouri River. In the last twenty years, the town becoming an enclave of artists and creatives flocking to the small city for affordable living, fresh air to breathe, and space to create among like-minded people. It's no Eureka Springs in Arkansas, but she was making her mark in the Missouri area. Boonville still had a mixture of old-timers living out their days along the mighty Missouri River and young families moving into the area for the slower pace away from urban life. But Charlie knew about the underbelly of the city through his father. A religious community called The Source had been causing problems in the little town for years.

Jim Tanner was Charlie's father and pastor of First Baptist Church of Kansas City. Not only was Jim the lead pastor, but he also ran an organization that investigated cults and provided abuse counseling for their victims. Jim had commissioned Charlie to drop off the youth group kid's in Boonville for camp. He then was going to join Charlie a day later and check out a lead on some activity related to The Source. Jim believed this would be real-world ministry experience and help Charlie in his future vocation. Charlie saw it as an opportunity to meet some crazy people and have marvelous stories to tell his buddies back home.

The Source was a community that had roots all the way back to the Civil War. Jim had become obsessed with the group when a woman came to his office years ago for counseling. When he did some research of his own, it had become his White Whale. A cult Jim wanted nothing more than to see leave the earth. But The Source was stubborn and would not slip quietly into the night.

Charlie glanced into the rear-view mirror about ten minutes into the trip. His speech didn't work. Greg Parker was licking his fingers and placing them in the ears of Jason Caldwell. Jason turned and swung at Greg. Charlie smiled, thinking back to just a couple of years earlier, making the same trek to Hickory Hill. He'd gotten a wedgie from Wyatt Smithson and hung by his underwear on the back of a cabin door. Charlie vowed never to attend church camp in any capacity. *But here we are.*

He ignored the minor rumble in the backseat—Charlie's thoughts meandering to his future and the pressure of being the next pastor in training. For years, Jim Tanner had dreams of his oldest child taking over the family business. But Charlie had other interests. A creative who loved to make music and write stories. The idea of being a pastor or counselor sounded like death. He'd rather be locked in his room telling stories or working on his guitar licks. Charlie had also been around enough religious people and found many of them selfish and fickle.

The music is too loud. Sermons are long and boring. Not enough programs or we do too many. We don't reach out to the community; we do too much. What about our needs? The church is too political or not political enough. Charlie had seen his dad take many arrows from church people and wanted none of it.

Charlie yelled from the driver's seat, "Greg, please stop putting your fingers in Jason's ears." Greg gave a thumbs up, licked his fingers, and did it again.

That's about right, Charlie thought to himself. *How can I have any authority in these kids' lives when we went to the same high school last year?* Charlie tried to find the positive side and knew the mission was simple. Get the kids to camp in one piece. Wait for Dad to arrive the next day, and help with whatever weird cult stuff is going down, head home, and then pick the kids up in a week. And hopefully have some cool stories to tell his buddies.

Charlie knew the summer job as a pastor in training wouldn't be all that bad. At least he could make some money and keep gas in the car. Maybe take a girl to a movie. Also, pastor work was less physically draining compared to installing decks with Uncle Richard like last summer. The flexibility of pastor life made space for other creative pursuits, a plus too.

The noise in the back of the van ramped up. Charlie changed strategies and determined he'd stay quiet and not try to bother the teens. As long as they started no fires, farting left to a minimum, he'd make the ninety minute drive with sanity intact. Charlie put in earbuds and cranked up a podcast. He'd been enjoying a show about the creative process of artists. He knew one episode would get him to Boonville.

The van rumbled east on highway seventy, and the density of the city gave way to the sparse barrenness of the country. Strip malls and dealerships were replaced with open spaces, cattle, and horses. Cars packed together dispersed as the church van moved closer to Boonville. Only a few cars littered the highway. Charlie lost track of time listening to the podcast. An artist living in Switzerland talked about the proper temperature for blowing glass. He thought one day he'd like to visit Europe.

Heaviness weighed on Charlie's eyelids as the van was finally quiet and the road noise hypnotic. Boonville was only about ten miles away. The stress of the morning and the struggle to be honest with Dad about not wanting to be a pastor sat in the pit of his stomach. Charlie pulled off seventy highway and headed right toward highway sixty-seven, a two-lane. The pavement turned to gravel.

Charlie heard laughter from the back of the van. Someone had ripped a big fart, and Greg Parker lost his mind. A girl covered her face with a pillow, and another propped a side window open and sucked in the fresh air.

Charlie couldn't help but smile, putting himself in the place of the teens only twelve months earlier. Wyatt Smithson ripped a few good ones on the trip to camp last summer.

Sticking to his strategy of silence. Charlie heard the music of his podcast cueing the end of the show. He clicked off the podcast and noticed only five minutes until arrival, according to his app.

He sighed and felt relief ending the first leg of the journey with minimal problems. A few farts and Wet Willy's were not the worst things in the world. The sooner Charlie got back home, the better.

Charlie snapped the case shut on his earbuds. He turned his head to tell the group they were only a few minutes away.

A scream rang from the back of the van. A girl yelled something intelligible.

Before Charlie could turn back toward the road, darkness, a deer had leaped into view without warning.

Home, a distant memory.

Chapter Two

The late morning sun reflected off bent metal. A crow squawked in the distance—the First Baptist Church of Kansas City fifteen-passenger van laid on its side. Gas and the odors of burnt brake pads wafted into the Missouri sky. Deer blood dripped off the windshield. A clot of deer fur lodged in the front grill of the Ford van.

Charlie blinked a couple of times, awakening from his sleep. *Is this a dream?* He caressed his flannel shirt and tapped on his chest. *Am I alive? Is this heaven?*

He unstrapped his seat belt and pushed on the van door, not realizing they were on their side. It opened skyward, and Charlie winced as the sun burned his eyes. He climbed out of the van and slump to the gravel floor. Blinding pain shot down the right side of his body. Ribs, hip, neck, and right ankle were throbbing with pain. *Had we flipped?*

Charlie scanned the quiet two-lane highway and examined the bent up van. It hadn't even occurred to him at this point that a van full of teenagers laid on its side. His memory of the last two hours was fuzzy, and pieces of the events were flashing like a movie rebooting multiple times.

He ran to the back of the van and yelled for the kids. It seemed appropriate as his vague memories included teenagers. No answer.

Charlie then climbed the side of the van to peer into the windows. The pain in attempting the spider man climb up the side of the van almost forced Charlie to faint. He banged on the windows and yelled for the teens.

No answer.

His memories vague and spotty, flashing in and out like random pieces of paper with partial messages. *Was this a dream? Are teenagers part of the dream, or not?*

No kids. But for whatever reason, the impulse of finding the teens seemed to confirm in Charlie's mind it was important.

Charlie slid down the side of the van and limped to the back. He noticed the back door of the van swung open. *Maybe I was knocked out for a while, and the teens went for help?* He peeked inside the van and yelled one more time despite not seeing a soul.

Did someone take them?

Charlie wobbled on the verge of losing consciousness. The pain in his ankle and side ramped up in intensity. Charlie wanted to cry from the pain. But also wanted to cry because of how his dad was going to respond. That memory was becoming clear. He could hear him now. *You had one job to do, get the teens to camp. And you couldn't even do that.*

Not to mention the mob of angry parents after apparently losing twelve teenagers on the back roads of Missouri.

Twelve? Were my memories coming back?

Charlie walked to the edge of the gravel road and glanced back and forth down the highway. Not a car in sight and only the sound of a crow in the distance. He remembered his cell phone in the van. Unfortunately, it would require another spider man crawl to retrieve the device. He fought through the blinding pain and found the phone with one bar of juice left.

The only person to call was the one who held the future of his young life in his hands, Dad. Charlie sighed and gave a brief prayer to the heavens. He dialed the number and waited.

Voicemail.

Dad, it's Charlie. I'm in a bit of trouble. Don't be alarmed. I'm okay. I got in an accident.

Charlie walked in the gravel and saw the demolished deer carcass on the ground. *We hit a deer, and I crashed the van. I'm fine... and the kids are fine. I'm just off highway sixty-seven near Boonville. Please call me back soon. I don't know what to do.*

Almost on cue, a Ford-350 blasting country music with smoke stacks and a rumbling diesel engine pulled up next to the mangled van. A heavy-set balding man with a sleeve of tattoos, earrings, and dark sunglasses leaned out the driver's window.

"Need some help? Your van has seen better days."

Charlie hung his head in shame. "Yeah, I hit a deer. I called for help but got no answer," Charlie said, with his cell phone still in hand.

"Want a lift? Town is only a few miles up the road. I can drop you at the police station. They'll take care of you."

Charlie stared at the man and hesitated to answer. The man looked confused after making the kind gesture. Charlie wasn't comfortable taking a ride with a stranger. Let alone a stranger with tattoos and a gun mounted in the cab. *And what if Dad came to pick me up? He's already going to be steaming hot. He shows up, and I'm gone. I'll never leave my bedroom. What other options do I have?*

Weighing heavily in his mind was the reality that twelve teenagers vanished. They were his responsibility, and Charlie let many people down.

Charlie glanced at his phone, now telling him low battery. "My phone is about to die. If you can get me to the police station. I'll try to call my folks one more time."

"Hop in, partner. How rude of me. Name's Roger. But my friends call me Snake. I'd say we're friends now."

Charlie reached out for the hand of the gloved driver. A little uncomfortable with the friend talk, knowing he could end his life with the flick of a finger. But desperate times call for desperate measures. "Charlie Tanner. I'm from Kansas City and really appreciate your help."

"My pleasure."

Snake slammed the gas pedal, and the diesel engine rumbled through the quiet roads, nearing Boonville. Charlie glanced out the window into the open spaces and farms, trying to contemplate his next move. The sign for Boonville popped up near a turn on the highway. "Boonville: Happiness is Our Last Name."

Charlie thought that was a strange motto for a small town. Too much like Disneyland for his taste. "Funny sign. You originally from Boonville?" Charlie asked.

"Yes, sir. The happiest place in the world. We aren't mighty in numbers, but big on happiness. The best place to live on the planet."

Charlie smirked. "You think so? What's so great about Boonville?"

Snake gripped his chin with one hand and steered with the other. "Let me count the ways. The people, for one. Nicest people in the world. They always have each other's back no matter what. Raised my entire family here in Boonville. My parents, grandparents, all from here. My wife and all her family. We could've left a long time ago. But why leave our little slice of paradise?"

"I heard Switzerland is nice," Charlie said, under his breath.

"What was that?"

"Nothing. I just don't think Boonville made the Top Ten of desirable places to live in America. You can't say it's the best if you've lived nowhere else. Kansas City is cool."

"KC is fine. Everyone has their opinion. But I bet you hang around our people long enough, and your opinions will change."

Charlie ignored the comment and felt the pain in his body move from the right side to his head. A giant headache formed in the front of his brain. He winced in the leather bucket seats of the truck as it bumped along. Snake peeked over, "Nasty wreck back there. Glad you're okay. You need anything?"

"I guess it could be worse. But my body feels like someone smacked me with a bag of nickels. I could use some Advil."

"I remember playing football for Boonville High. Every Saturday morning after the game. I felt like squirrels with boxing gloves had punched me a million times. I don't have any Advil. Do you need to see a doctor?"

Charlie rubbed his side. "I'll be okay for now. My ribs are super tender."

Snake cruised down Main Street in Boonville and pulled up to the front of the police station. He unlocked the door and gave a toothy grin. "Great meeting you, kid. Sheriff John Brown will take good care of you. Tell em' Snake sent ya. Get those ribs looked at."

Charlie nodded and climbed out of the truck. He limped to the entrance of the police station and entered the sliding doors. He wobbled to the desk where a brunette sat answering phones. "Can I see Sheriff John Brown?"

She told Charlie to take a seat, and the sheriff would be with him in a minute.

Boonville

Charlie did everything he could not to black out.

Chapter Three

Sheriff John Brown placed his boots on the desk and puffed a cigar. Charlie held in a laugh as the sheriff reminded him of Uncle Larry. An Uber religious conservative that made for interesting Thanksgiving dinners. He smoked cigars like kids eating candy on Halloween until lung cancer got him.

The walls of the office were covered in taxidermy and gold plaques of various awards. Sheriff Brown turned in his swivel chair and faced Charlie. "So my secretary says you're in a pinch. Snake also confirmed as much. Well, you came to the right place. Boonville is all about helping people."

Charlie sensed an inauthenticity in the sheriff's voice. Like he's said this to every person he meets but doesn't mean a word. But Charlie didn't have time to worry about the integrity of the sheriff as he needed a phone and wanted to contact his father and get home.

Charlie caught himself staring at a deer's head, which appeared to be stalking him with his eyes. "Uh, yeah, good to hear. What you can help me with is a phone. You wouldn't happen to have a cell phone charger? I seem to have lost mine," Charlie said, holding up his now dead cell.

"We're old school around here—no cell phones. I have a landline you can use. Will that work?"

"Yes, sir."

"What brings you to our corner of paradise? Charlie is it?"

Charlie nodded. "Charlie Tanner."

"Snake mentioned you had a little bit of a fender bender."

"Fender bender? Yeah, I've been in a fender bender. A fender bender on steroids. Did Snake tell you our van flipped, and I'm lucky to be alive?"

Sheriff Brown leaned over the wide oak desk. His breath wreaked of cigar smoke. A nasty smell like the cigars Uncle Larry smoked. "I'm so sorry, kid. Was anyone hurt?"

"Besides me? I don't know," Charlie said, contemplating whether to tell the sheriff about the missing teens.

"You don't know? Was anyone riding with you?"

"I'm fine. But yes, I had passengers. They, uh, appear to be missing."

Confessing the missing teens sounded otherworldly coming from the mouth of Charlie. *How can kids vanish in thin air? Maybe they snuck out of the back and ran for help? They'll turn up in town soon.*

"Missing? I've heard some whoppers in my day, but this is a gem," the sheriff said, taking a puff on the cigar, "How many people we talking?"

"I'm telling the truth, I think. My memory is fuzzy."

Charlie scratched the side of his head and nervously bounced his feet on the ground. But quickly stopped, feeling the pain in his battered ankle shoot up his leg. "Twelve teens."

"Twelve?" Brown asked, tapping cigar ash out in an ashtray. "I'd say that's a problem. Where do you think they went?"

Charlie shrugged. "I hit a deer. I must've blacked out. When I came too, the van was toast, and my crew was missing. Weird, I know. Did anyone call the station?"

The sheriff smiled through his yellowed teeth. "I think if twelve kids are missing, we'd know about it. Maybe you have a concussion. Should we send you to a doctor?"

"I'm not lying. My memory is fuzzy, but there were kids in the van. Can I make that call? I think my dad can help and clear things up. He was coming up tomorrow, anyway."

Sheriff Brown could see Charlie was getting amped up. He held up his chunky hands. "Calm down, kid. We'll figure this out. I just think your memory might fail you. What brings you and your dad to Boonville?"

"Long story short. I was taking some high school kids to Camp Hickory Hill for the week. It's a Christian youth camp."

The sheriff nodded. "Oh yes, we know the Hickory Hill people. Andy Williams runs that fine camp. Good people. Been doing the Lord's work for fifty years in our town. Why was your dad coming up to visit?"

"Business. It's complicated."

"I'm in the loop of most of the happenings in this town. No mentions about any new business in town. What kind of business are you talking about?"

Describing what Charlie's dad did for work wasn't easy. "Counseling. My dad helps people hurt by cults. I guess there's a cult in the area: The Source or something. I don't know much about it. Can I make that call?" Charlie said, reaching for the outdated phone perched on the desk.

The sheriff slammed his aging paw on Charlie's hand. His blue eyes pierced through his body. "Boonville is a proud town with proud people. Happiness is our last name. We love having new people come and visit our piece of paradise. But don't be snooping around people you know nothing about."

Charlie tried to slip his hand away from the grip of the sheriff. He leaned back in the chair. "I'm sorry. I honestly don't know much about my dad's work. I'm sure they're fine people. I meant nothing by it. I just want to find my dad and our group."

Sheriff John Brown's countenance turned as he switched to a whisper. He smashed the remnants of the cigar in a glass ashtray and leaned back in his chair. "Your story sounds a little bit fishy. I've been working in law enforcement for thirty years and heard nothing like this. Kids don't go missing after a crash. I'll send a tow truck and get your van back into town. Please make your call and tell your father not to do anything he'd regret."

The sheriff rose from his chair and walked to the other side of the desk. He pointed a finger at Charlie's chest. "Don't be snooping in places you don't belong. You, or your dad. Got it?" he said, lightly slapping Charlie on the side of his head.

Charlie felt a chill in his words, and the room shrank. The inauthenticity in the exchange with the sheriff came back. But wanted nothing more than to leave and leave fast. "Yes, sir. No problem. I'm going to make that call and get out of your way."

Sheriff Brown stood upright and acted as if nothing happened. "Good. How about a place to stay for the night? I'll call the Boonville Hotel and get you a room. They'll take good care of you. You like cheeseburgers? Best burger in town right next door."

Charlie fiddled with the phone and glanced at the sheriff. "I'm super hungry, thank you."

Charlie called his dad and got the voicemail for a second time. He left a message.

He wondered why his dad wasn't answering the phone. It wasn't like him to go silent for so long. *Is this all a dream?*

Chapter Four

An officer in the Boonville Police Department dropped Charlie off in front of the Boonville Hotel. A two-story building with original brick on the front and a quaint handwritten sign saying: the best hotel in town.

Charlie was certain it was the only hotel in town. It was only half a block from the police department, and it seemed silly to drive. Most of the hot spots in Boonville appeared to be on one long block on Main Street. Ice cream shop, restaurants, bars, lawyer office, toy store, and hardware store. The end of the street butting up next to the Missouri River.

Charlie thanked the gangly police officer, who gave a wry smile. He reflected on the conversation with Sheriff Brown, and the only word coming to mind was creepy. Everything that came out of the mouth of the sheriff was dripping with dishonesty, like a used car sales associate Charlie and his dad encountered years ago when replacing the family minivan. Dad told Charlie to be careful of guys like the sheriff. They bring you in with their plastic smiles while in the back; they steal your wife and your money. The sheriff also was causing doubt in Charlie's mind that everything that happened was a dream or made up. Regardless, Charlie was hungry and wanted nothing more than to contact his dad.

The front desk of the Boonville Hotel was a monstrosity that spanned the entire width of the lobby. Charlie thought it was disproportionate to the size of the hotel. Nobody was in the lobby, and a young girl tapped on a computer at the desk.

Charlie paused at the beauty of the architecture in the lobby. An arch spanned across the ceiling with unfinished wood. A couple rustic ceiling fans spun in time. He'd always loved architecture, spending years visiting churches with his dad. Regardless of the nonsense in many churches, the buildings were pieces of art.

Charlie limped to the front desk. A girl looked up from a monitor on the desk. Charlie thought it was odd that she was furiously typing despite not one soul in the lobby. "Are you the accident kid?"

Charlie smiled. "Word gets around fast in Boonville. I am the accident kid. But I'm eighteen, not sure if that counts as a kid?"

The girl tapped on the keyboard and returned a smile. "Nice to see someone in my age bracket. I'm a year older. But most people in this town are old geezers. Sweet people, but mostly older. The hipsters are moving in, which is bringing the average age down. Nice to see someone else besides drunk bikers riding through town or families on their way to somewhere else."

"Well, I'm glad I can help with the demographics in this place."

The girl was caught off guard by the comment. "Why? Is Boonville weird?"

"I know your last name is happiness. But I get a weird vibe around here."

"Yeah, a little Disney-ish for my taste. It'll grow on you. How can I help you? My name is Katie."

"Charlie. But shouldn't you have known that? I'm the accident kid, remember?" Charlie said with a wink.

"Yes, Sheriff Brown mentioned it. I have a room booked for the night. Is it just you?"

Charlie spun around and inspected the empty lobby. "Uh, no. Actually, three guests. Me, myself, and I."

"Funny," Katie said in a monotone voice. "Breakfast is at 7 AM. It's free for all our guests. No Wi-Fi."

Charlie nodded. "I'd take internet over the Continental Breakfast any day. I remember traveling with my dad and eating three bowls of Fruit Loops at a Holiday Inn. I puked in the car."

"We don't have Fruit Loops. But it's all you can eat."

Charlie liked Katie. Despite her straightforward answers, he could tell behind her brown eyes was a sweet girl. He could see himself hanging out with her and having a fun time.

"What do you suppose I do in this town with no internet?" Charlie asked with a hint of sarcasm.

"I don't know. Read a book. It won't kill you."

Charlie held up his hands. "As you can tell. I'm traveling light. It would've been nice to catch up on my Netflix queue."

Katie slid a room key across the desk. "Sorry. You're in room 12."

Charlie shook his head.

"Is there a problem?" Katie asked, staring down at the key.

"It's nothing. The number twelve has some negative memories."

"The twelve kids that are missing?" Katie shot back.

Charlie stepped back from the front desk in shock. "How do you know about that?"

"Word travels fast," Katie said. She opened a drawer in the

desk and yanked out a Sticky Note. She then glanced up toward the ceiling. "I'm also instructed to feed you. I get off in an hour. Head over to the restaurant next door—best cheeseburger in town. I'll tell you more. Call me if you need anything. Careful, they're watching us."

Charlie slid the key off the desk and into his pocket. Right then, a man came rushing through the door. He was carrying a black duffel bag. The older man with a potbelly and overalls slung the bag next to Charlie's feet.

"We're working on your van. Found this inside. I'm assuming these are your things."

Charlie examined the bag and confirmed. "Yes, thank you, sir. Any other items in the van?"

The man held up a cell phone charger. "Just this."

Charlie grabbed the charger. "Thank you. How is the van?"

The man then rushed out of the hotel and didn't say a word.

Katie held her arms crossed. "I told you. Meet me an hour, and we'll talk more."

Charlie went to his room, set an alarm on his charging phone, and fell asleep. More than anything, Charlie wanted to wake up and realize all of this was a dream.

Chapter Five

Bells rang in the distance. Charlie thought he had a dream about a church burning down in a small town like Boonville. With a sweaty face and heart pumping, Charlie slammed his hand on the phone, shutting off the alarm. He inspected the room of the Boonville Hotel. Bad art of a clown hanging above the bed, check. Hunger pangs, check. And massive amounts of pain running through his battered body, check.

He reached for the Sticky Note from Katie on the end table. Charlie texted: *Please bring Advil, my head is killing me. We still good for dinner?*

Katie quickly responded: *yes, and yes.*

The mattress of the sleigh bed felt hard as Charlie sat on the edge. He wondered how many guests came through the Boonville Hotel in a given year. He then dialed his dad.

Voicemail.

Charlie, frustrated with the silence of Dad, had a revelation. *Why not call mom?* June Tanner was more accommodating and gracious in situations like these. Charlie always went to Mom first when asking to spend the night at a friend's house or begging for an extra bowl of cereal. Dad was often a quick *no*.

Mom didn't answer, either. Charlie left a voicemail.

My mom lives on her phone. Texting friends. Scrolling Facebook. The one time you need them, they don't pick up. Really?

Charlie shook off the nap, wobbled into the bathroom, and took a leak. He then stared into the mirror, examining the cuts and bruises on the side of his face. A purplish hue formed on his cheek. He held up his flannel shirt and examined the bruising on the right side of his ribs. *Not good.*

He splashed cold water on his face, tucked in his shirt, and headed down to the restaurant to meet Katie. It was late afternoon, and the temps were unusually high for June in Missouri.

Charlie exited the hotel and walked one building to the right. Max's. A diner like something belonging in the 50s. Juke box, red plastic booths, and mostly burgers and fries on the menu. Charlie's stomach grumbled as he opened the door and was blasted with Buddy Holly on the jukebox.

Katie sat in a booth across the restaurant, scrolling her phone and stirring a Coke with a straw. Charlie sat down as the booth squeaked from the plastic material. "Good seeing you here."

"Nice hair," Katie shot back, then slid Advil across the table. "Here are your drugs."

Charlie brushed the side of his hair, realizing he gave little attention to his bed head. "Thanks for the drugs. And what's wrong with my hair? It's how the cool kids wear it these days. I didn't realize this was an *actual* date. I should've used some gel in my duffle bag."

Katie sipped her Coke and then said nonchalantly. "Not a date. You're not my type. I don't date vagabonds riding through town unannounced. I'm not that kind of girl."

"What kind of girl are you?" Charlie asked, trying to break through the hard veneer of Katie.

Katie leaned in close over the sticky surface of the diner table. She whispered, "Doesn't matter. Let's talk about the guy that returned your bag. Was it coincidental that a man with your things showed up when he did? Right when I handed you the note? Weird, right?"

Charlie shrugged, feeling his stomach do a flip because of hunger. "I'm starving. So, yeah, it's a little weird. Or, maybe, it just happens a nice man working on my van returned my things so I could get a good night's sleep. Possible?"

"Anything is possible. I could also get hit by an asteroid in the next five minutes. Possible, but not likely. They're watching us. They're always watching us."

"Who are *they*? You're not a right-wing conspiracy theorist person, are you? I've seen enough of that stuff on YouTube. I'll admit, Boonville has a Twin Peaks vibe. But let's not get crazy here."

"No crazy here, my vagabond friend. This is actual life. They've been stalking us ever since my family moved into town."

"Can you please tell me who *they* are? And if you're being watched. I'm not a lawyer. But that's a crime. You can call the police. You want me to call Boonville PD? I know the sheriff," Charlie said, holding up his phone.

"What if the police are watching us? The unofficial police of Boonville. They've made that clear the minute we unpacked the U-Haul years ago."

"What if what you're saying is true? A big *if*. Which, by the way, sounds a little nutty. Why not just call the police? Or better yet, why not leave?"

"Good question, and it's not that simple. My oldest sister got a scholarship to Missouri University about six years ago.

Melissa was the first to go to college in our family. My dad had just lost his job in Florida and had no prospects. He thought it was time for a change of pace. We'd live near Melissa while she worked through school. So we moved to Boonville. That's at least how my parents justify it."

"You miss the ocean?"

Katie finished her soda. "Did you hear anything I said? I explained how we ended up in this crazy town, and all you got was I'm from Florida?"

"No, I'm with you. I just have a thing for oceans."

"Why? Did you date one or something?"

"Oh, you're a comedian now. I just think the culture of beach towns are fascinating. Some of the best music has come from the coasts. I'm a big fan of the Beach Boys."

"What are you sixty years old?"

"I've always believed I grew up in the wrong generation. The Beach Boys were the only secular music we could listen to growing up."

"Religious home?" Katie asked.

"Very. Dad's a pastor, doesn't get more religious than that. You?"

"Yep. We had Johnny Cash. Only the gospel albums. Religious homes aren't the best places for discovering good music. That's what older siblings are for. I discovered the good stuff later."

"Amen, sister. I found the good music, not from a sibling, but from friends. But I'm going out on a limb here. Did the move have something to do with religion?"

Katie stared down at the bottom of her empty soda and played with the straw. A server in a poodle skirt skated up to the table. "What you want, love birds?"

"It's not like that," Charlie shot back. "I'll take the Elvis Burger with extra pickles. Onion rings."

"Same, no rings, fries, thanks," Katie said, avoiding eye contact with Charlie. "Awkward, right? Thinking we're on a date. You're not my type, remember?" she forced a smirk.

Charlie sensed Katie opening up and putting down her guard. "Sorry about the religion stuff. It's none of my business. I know that can be a sensitive subject."

"It *is* your business. I'm the weird girl that invited you to a restaurant to talk about people watching us. We're way beyond awkward."

"Trust me, I know, awkward. My dad works with religious people. I've sampled versions of your story before. Family moves from a big city to escape the hustle and bustle—a new start. Find themselves in a small town in the middle of nowhere. They find a religious community, and they become an extended family. Rarely makes sense to a watching world. Unless you've experienced it."

Katie nodded and then blurted out, "I've heard of your dad's work."

"Wait, what? How do you know my dad?"

"I don't know him, know him. Heard the name, Jim Tanner. I won't tell anyone you're related. Let's say he's not popular in these parts."

"Please explain."

"I have my sources. Word gets around fast in a small town like Boonville."

"Was it the sheriff? He doesn't like me."

"When Sheriff Brown called to set up your room. I recognized the name. Thought you might work for the enemy."

Charlie felt the top of his head getting warm. "You know nothing about me or my family. We're not the enemy. My dad isn't trying to hurt people, only help. I don't even know what my dad is doing here. I just want to go home."

Katie reached for the hand of Charlie. He glanced up,

surprised by the gesture. "Hey, I'm the one who invited you here. I was only joking. Your father isn't the enemy. I'm trying to help you. All I know is this town has demons. And I want those demons exercised."

"Why should I trust you? Or anyone in this town? The sheriff sure didn't rank high on the trust meter."

"Cross my heart and hope to die. I'm in your corner. I don't have all the details. But your dad came to town last year and claimed one of our community members was being abused. He got the local authorities involved and tried to have our supreme leader arrested to no avail. Our community doesn't like people holding them accountable. That's how your pops officially became an enemy of our town."

Charlie leaned back in his chair, trying to take in everything that Katie dropped in his lap. "Is your little religious community the ones watching us? Are they bad people?"

Katie nodded. "Bad? I don't know. But the day we landed in the city of 'happiness is our last name,' I knew it was a lie. I'm certain people in this town have drunk the Kool-Aid on a massive scale. Including Sheriff John Brown. He's part of our community. And what I heard isn't fond of your father."

"Remind me why I should believe any of this? Aren't you drinking the Kool-Aid too? This town has been more than odd since the minute I flipped that van. I'm just trying to make sense of what happened, make things right, and get home."

The server delivered their plates of food. Charlie dug into the burger and downed a handful of fries.

"Let's finish our food. I'll show you why you can trust me," Katie said.

Chapter Six

Katie paid the bill at Max's and left a generous tip. Charlie thought that said a lot about Katie, despite her edge. She told Charlie to follow her down an alley between the Boonville Hotel and the Max's. Her car was parked in the back.

They peeled out, and Charlie held onto the inside handle of a Honda Civic. His heart pumping as Katie drove with wild abandon.

Charlie yelled above the engine noise. "Where are we going? And can you please slow down? I'd like to see my nineteenth birthday."

Katie jammed her foot further into the gas pedal and rarely watched the road. "You want to know why I'm here? You want to know what your dad came to do? I'm going to show you."

Katie gunned the Honda as the four-cylinder engine revved beyond its capacity. The car smelled of burning plastic. Main Street disappeared, and in a few minutes, they were out in the country on a windy road. Shops and buildings replaced with farm houses, wide-open spaces, as the smell of fresh-cut grass. A mower purred in the distance.

Katie rolled down her window, and the warm air of Missouri in June came into the car. For a moment, Charlie felt peace despite the chaos of his trip to Boonville.

Katie navigated turns and also navigated a worn CD case laying in between the seats. Charlie was simultaneously impressed and terrified, praying the compact car didn't slam into a guardrail or go into the ditch.

"Need help with that?" Charlie asked.

"Nope," Katie said, ripping the case free from the seat.

"Who still listens to CD's and uses a CD player? A dinosaur called and wants his music back," Charlie said, still hanging on for dear life in the speeding Honda.

"Be quiet. I'm lucky to even have a car. You said you like the Beach Boys, right?"

Katie popped in Pet Sounds and cranked up the volume. Still oblivious to the road and the human life sitting next to her.

Charlie was in love. Not only did Katie own a Beach Boys CD, but she possessed, in his opinion, the best album ever made. "Whatever I thought of you before has now vanished. Pet Sounds? You have no idea what this means to me. Pet Sounds is the best album ever. Rivals any Beatles record. Most rock-and-roll historians suggest the Beatles wrote Sergeant Peppers based on Pet Sounds. The mop tops from the UK said the Beach Boys created the most forward-thinking album of all time. Which, of course, it is."

"That's a lot of information... nerd. I just like how it sounds."

"Like heaven," Charlie said, snapping along to Sloop John B. "Where are we going again?"

"You'll see. Just enjoy the music and my driving."

"I'll take one and leave the other. I sweated through my shirt."

The sun had set, and the lights of Boonville were off in the distance. Katie turned down Pet Sounds as the Honda rolled up in front of a Catholic Church. The white-pillared building sat perched on a hill overlooking Boonville. No life inside. Katie pointed from the driver's window.

"See that place? That's where it all goes down."

"Are you Catholic?"

"No. That's where all the weird cult stuff goes down."

Charlie leaned back in the passenger seat. He scratched his head. "You never said you belonged to a cult. Just a religious community? That can mean a lot of things."

"Come on, smarty pants. If your dad's involved, you know it has to be a cult. Here's the crazy thing about cults. When you're in one, you don't know until you do. Your dad would agree."

Charlie gave a forced smile. He could sense the pain in Katie's voice hidden behind the jokes. "So what goes *down* in this place? Child sacrifice? The slaughtering of goats?"

Katie punched Charlie in the arm. "Not exactly. Want to hear a cool story?"

"Always."

"This building used to be owned by a Roman Catholic Church. About fifty years ago, there was a mine fire. The fire department spent millions of dollars trying to put out the underground fire. But they couldn't. The fire is still burning underground today. You can see the smoke rise under the pavement in the daylight."

Charlie folded his arms. "Get out of here. A fire under the ground?"

"Yep, it's a thing. I couldn't make this stuff up. You can only imagine the teachings The Source built around a fire burning under the city. A fire burning under their place of worship and why it never goes out. Experts say it can burn for another hundred years."

"Did you say The Source?"

"Yes, sir. That's our cult, I mean religious community," Katie said.

"My memory isn't so great since the crash. But I remember Dad saying something about The Source. I thought it would be a cool band name."

"They have a thing for music. Our leader is a musician and shares many of his songs that have come straight from the mouth of God. Let me say, they're no Pet Sounds."

"So what kind of stuff goes on in the building? Do people live here?"

"Nobody lives here. Services are held here every Sunday. We have a compound where other teachings and activities happen. The main leader Zebediah Mulvaney apparently has a small apartment in the building. You can imagine the rumors swirling around what goes down in that apartment."

"Zebediah? Please tell me that's a joke. How can any rational person follow a dude with a name like that?"

"Like I said. You don't know you're in a cult until you're in one."

"Can we go inside? I want to see the smoke rising from the ground."

"Are you crazy, Charlie? You're lucky I even brought you here. If I get caught, bad things are coming my way. Most likely for helping you out."

Charlie gazed at the Roman Catholic Church building, now turned cult facility. "Well, for what it's worth. I appreciate your help in whatever mess I've found myself in Boonville. Can I ask a serious question?"

"Better not be rock-and-roll trivia."

"It's not. And by the looks of your CD collection, a waste of time. Why are you so indifferent about The Source? Are you still involved? Is your family?"

"A great and confusing question. It's complicated. We allow every Source member when they turn eighteen, a hiatus. Which means you have an option to leave the community for a year. You're not expected to take part in the community's life for twelve months. Have time to see the big wicked world. But after the year is up, you have two choices. One, come back to The Source for a lifetime and give your full allegiance. Two, or get excommunicated. Never to return. I have six months to decide. It's like what the Amish call *Rumspringa*."

"I'm no prophet. But I'm guessing you're leaving The Source after the six months, right?"

Katie's eyes welled up. She stared at the building. "I've considered all my options. You probably think I'm crazy for even considering staying with the community. But these crazy people are my family. And in our doctrine, if you leave the community, you're disowned by your biological family. You can see the pickle I find myself in," Katie said, with a tear sliding down her cheek. She wiped it clear.

Charlie glared at the building. Anger rising up at the thought of Katie being shunned by her family. He stayed silent.

"What am I supposed to do? Everything isn't bad at The Source. I have a loving extended family. Predictability with a shared common life. A job. I don't like the arranged marriage thing. But I have my eye on a couple prospects," she said with a smile.

"Arranged marriage? What are you talking about? A beautiful girl like you forced to marry some dude in a cult? I don't think so. You sound like many of the people my dad works with. He's worked with enough people to say these cults are nothing good and *all* evil."

Katie hung her head against the steering wheel. "I just wish my family never moved here. I wish I wasn't forced with an impossible decision."

"It doesn't have to be this way. Who can I talk to?"

"Talk to? You don't just walk into our community and start accusing people of stuff. That's why your dad is on the enemy list."

"Sometimes you have to speak the truth in love. Can I talk to your folks? Maybe join a meeting and talk some sense into these people?"

"I appreciate the gesture, but it doesn't work like that. Trust me. No amount of persuasion is going to change anyone's minds. Cults are dogmatic. And dogma is virtually impossible to change. We need to work on getting you back home."

"I got nothing but time. Why not do some good while we wait?"

"Ironically, there's a meeting down the road as we speak. It's a midweek teaching night."

Charlie reached across the dashboard and ripped the keys out of the ignition. He opened the door, limped to the driver's side, and told Katie to get out. "Get in the passenger side. We're going on a field trip. Have some cult fun."

Katie braced herself in the driver's seat. "Charlie, this isn't a game. Jebediah doesn't like anyone messing with our community. I'm telling you, Boonville is not what you think it is."

Charlie opened the door and ushered Katie to the other side of the car. "My dad always says. Let things be what they need to be. I think we need to make a brief visit. You can stay in the car. I'll pretend I'm interested in the group. Talk to a few people and bail."

"Fine, it's your funeral," Katie said, shaking her head. "Just don't tell them your name is Tanner. You won't see that birthday."

Chapter Seven

Charlie pulled into the parking lot, got out of the car to stretch, and then stood outside the car. He scanned to the left to what appeared to be horse stables. The Source compound a former camp for taking care of horses and other animals. A line of cabins, an admin building, playground, and basketball courts sprawled through the open campground. Plenty of space for the community to live out their days waiting for Armageddon.

Katie refused to come inside the meeting because of her hiatus. And she also had no desire to experience more of the same. Charlie promised to play it cool and not cause a ruckus. He'd be in and out—more of a curiosity mission.

Charlie limped up the gravel drive to the porch where the music played. He gently pushed and opened a metal double door. A young girl with pigtails greeted Charlie. She handed him a folded piece of paper for the teaching time. The girl was no older than thirteen. She had a long skirt and white sweater, which Charlie thought odd for June in Missouri. She reached out a hand and gave a wide smile.

"How are you? What brings you to The Source? Did someone invite you?"

Charlie returned the handshake. "Yeah, something like that. A friend said I should stop by. So here I am."

The girl hesitated and appeared to not have bought the half-truth. "Ok, well, good to meet you. The band is warming up. Get some coffee or punch in the corner. The cookies are also fresh out of the oven. If you have questions, let me know."

Charlie took in the place's vibe and reminded him of many church meetings he'd been at over the years. Music, chipper people, terrible coffee, and warm punch. Charlie thanked the girl and walked to grab a cup of coffee and a cookie. A jolt of energy welcomed as the day felt like an eternity.

He poured the coffee and doctored it up with cream and sugar. He'd hoped to mask the church coffee taste. Hunches confirmed. No amount of sugar was going to save the dark liquid. *You'd think as much coffee as church people drink, they'd invest in the good stuff. At least the cookies were warm.*

A guy in his twenties with a long goatee and built arms picked up an acoustic guitar and glided to the stage. The stage was only about a foot off the ground but fit nicely in proportion to the meeting space. Another guy jumped on drums, and a girl played bass. Charlie hoped for some Beach Boys covers in the rotation but knew that wasn't in the cards.

The guy with the guitar said, "Hey, Source family. Welcome to our midweek gathering. If you're visiting with us, so glad you stopped by. We're all about family, and we're all about love here. Zebediah has some special teaching worked up for you tonight. But before we start the teaching, let's sing a bit."

The band kicked in and didn't sound that bad. Not Beach Boys, but not terrible. Charlie scanned the room and noticed the diversity of the community. Young and old, black and white, and lots of small children. All swaying and lost in the music.

Charlie wasn't picking up cult vibes as the music played. Seemed like a friendly community of normal people. Nothing was done or said that appeared to be cultish. Charlie mused, *Not sure what problems Dad had with these folks?*

That was until Zebediah got up to speak.

A man with greying streaks in his dark hair, black-rimmed glasses, and blue jeans stepped onto the small stage. He opened a worn leather Bible and plopped it on a wooden pulpit, sighed, and appeared to be disturbed by something.

Zebediah paced the stage like a lion searching for prey. "Family, I had a message prepared tonight. But something in my spirit told me I needed to talk about something else. It appears we have resistance in our ranks. And if you're visiting tonight, I'm sorry we have to take care of some family business."

The crowd of about fifty gave an audible moan—each person scanning the room as if to find written across someone's head: resistor.

"You see, a family is like a body. And the body on the outside can look perfectly healthy. But without warning, a cancer can take over from the inside. Family, we have a cancer in our midst."

"Oh, no," shouted a woman.

Zebediah continued his speech. "Our forefathers fought a war to secure its freedoms. They died so we could live. They sacrificed their own freedom so a family like The Source could exist. But you see, these cancers come and try to destroy this beautiful thing we have. Destroy it from the inside out. We're not hurting anyone. And yet, they want to hurt us."

"Amen, brother," a man yelled.

Charlie placed his hands in his jean pockets. The room was

still. An intensity filled the space you could cut with a knife. Zebediah was an engaging speaker, and the participants hung on every word. His oration skills impressed Charlie, and he could see why someone might get sucked into a community like The Source.

But reality snuck into the back door. *Was this message aimed at my dad? Me?*

Charlie felt sweat pool up on his spine and drip down his jeans. The headache which disappeared after the Advil had returned in full force. The room spun, and Charlie's eyes were getting blurry.

"As you all know, Sheriff Brown, one of our original members in Boonville, keeps me apprised of any problems in our community. Well, he's updated me on some disappointing events in our Happy Town."

Charlie noticed a heavy-set man walking up the right side of the stage. He navigated between the guitar player and some other music equipment, stood next to Jebediah, and crossed his arms. The heavy man dressed in an all brown police uniform and ranger hat.

"I've asked Sheriff John Brown to address our community tonight," Jebediah said, handing the sheriff a microphone.

"I hate coming up here tonight under these circumstances. But it has come to my attention that someone doesn't like what we represent here in Boonville. They have come here to spread lies about this loving community. And we won't stand for it."

A voice yelled, "No way!"

"But here's the good news. We can have the cancer removed tonight. And we don't have to look very far."

Sheriff John Brown's eyes locked on Charlie. The jovial, chunky face of the sheriff turned to a scowl. His eyes narrowed, and he pointed a finger in Charlie's direction.

Charlie tried to keep it together. But the heat of the room, the intensity of the situation, and the pain in his body was no match for keeping his eyes open.

A girl next to him asked if he was okay. Charlie knew the face, the voice, and maybe a name.

Then everything went black.

Chapter Eight

Charlie heard beeping in the distance. A steady beep, beep, beep. He forced his eyes open. He then glanced to the right as the fogginess lifted from his head. An IV covered with a bandage jammed in his left forearm. He glanced down to a paper hospital gown. A face came into focus above the bed.

"You had a rough night, darling. I'm glad Sheriff Brown found you in that park. Things could've been much worse for you."

The story didn't resonate with Charlie. He searched for a memory in the back of his brain. He remembered a girl greeting him at the door of The Source meeting. Then he remembered a face. The face of a girl that was so familiar, and yet he couldn't make a concrete connection. "A girl. Who was the girl?" he said, with a gravelly voice.

"I'm sorry, honey. What girl? Yes, I am a girl."

"No, a girl. That girl, from the group," Charlie said, working hard to keep his eyes open. "Where am I? And who are you?"

"How rude of me. My name is Nurse Lucy. Lucy Harris. And you're in the finest medical facility in Boonville. Actually, the only medical facility in our town," she said with a giggle.

"Brown, Sheriff Brown. Where is he? I need to talk with him."

Lucy held up a skinny pointer finger with red nail polish. "You're in luck. He's right outside in the hallway. He saved your life last night."

Lucy left the room and spoke in hushed tones to Sheriff Brown standing in the hallway. Charlie's fog was lifting little by little. More clarity, but not much.

"Good morning, young man. I'm happy you're awake... and alive. It didn't look good last night," the sheriff said.

"What happened last night?"

"You don't remember? I found you in a park, passed out on a bench. I loaded you in the police cruiser. And here you are. Nurse Lucy has been watching you all night. Getting you better," he said, turning to the nurse, who gave a grin.

Something about the story didn't ring true and felt hallow. Charlie thought most of what the sheriff said landed sleazy and inauthentic. He remembered little from the night before but had a shadow of a memory of the sheriff, and it wasn't in a park. It was at a meeting with music. And the girl next to him kept swirling around in the recesses of his brain. "The girl. Who was the girl?"

The sheriff chuckled. "What girl? You were alone in the park. And, if I'm not mistaken, you were doing some naughty things. Things the laws in this town frown upon."

"Did I break the law? I don't remember ever being in a park. Let alone breaking laws. But I remember you and me at some meeting. And a girl with a familiar face."

"Nice try. If I was using drugs, I'd make up a contradicting story too. Last night I worked the night shift. Got a call of someone causing trouble in Brookside Park. Went and checked it out. I'm sure your mind is fuzzy after doing whatever drugs you're on."

Charlie was waking up and fighting through the convoluted memory. "Stop lying. You know who I am. I'm not using drugs. Unless you count, the Advil Katie gave me. I had a pounding headache, and Katie gave me some medicine and took me to a meeting. I don't remember all the details. But you were there, and another girl. A girl with a familiar face. Where's my van? I need to call my dad."

Sheriff John Brown asked the nurse to leave them alone. She obliged and pranced into the hallway. He took off his hat and placed it on a chair. His head was balding, and his teeth were yellow as he forced a fake smile.

"Yes, we've been acquainted. And I'm doing everything in my power to not lose my cool. We've done everything we can to get your van fixed. As far as the lost teens, well, that still seems like a fantasy not worth mentioning. You come into our town, and you take and take. We give and give. So please don't call me a liar. The real liar is obvious. I'm going to let the minor incident in the park go. But you're skating on thin ice, young man."

Charlie was in shock at the mini-lecture given by the sheriff. The ice in his words sent shivers down his spine. The sheriff almost convinced him he was on drugs. But Charlie would not relent. "Why don't you believe me? I saw a girl. I saw you. The kids are gone. Stop telling me what the truth is. I know what the truth is," Charlie said, fighting back a tear. He reached for the phone next to the bed, "I'm calling my dad. He'll make this right."

The sheriff ripped the cord out of the wall. "No! I call the shots around here. And right now, you ain't calling that man. He's a cancer."

The word cancer hung in the air. Charlie finally connected the dots of the night before. "Cancer... you and that weird cult leader talked about cancer. At the meeting you keep denying. You were there, and the girl was there, and music. There was no park."

Sheriff Brown held up his hands. "I'm sorry, I raised my voice. It's not what I'm about. It's not what Boonville is about. We want to err on the side of Happy. Here's what I'm going to do. I'll call Katie and get you back to the hotel. We'll keep working on the van and get you home. Sound like a plan?"

Charlie mumbled something and wanted nothing more than to leave the hospital and Brown. The idea of seeing Katie felt like the best news in the world. "Yeah, fine, whatever."

Charlie put on his clothes and said goodbye to nurse Lucy. Katie pulled up in front of the Boonville Hospital. Beach Boys played through the window.

"Where have you been?" Katie asked.

"I wish I knew."

Chapter Nine

Charlie jumped into the Honda and turned down the radio. He took a deep breath and unloaded. "I'm not sure what happened last night. But Sheriff Brown has lost his mind. Accused me of doing drugs. My mind isn't firing on all cylinders. What happened last night?"

"Take a breath, relax. The sheriff is crazy, that's not a new revelation. How did you end up at the hospital?" Katie asked.

"You don't know?"

"Come on, you seriously don't remember? You were persistent on going to The Source meeting. I waited in the car, and you went inside. The meeting ended, and the sheriff took you back to the Hotel."

"Are you sure?"

"The sheriff told me. He took you home on the way back to the precinct. Said it was on his way because he was on the night shift. What happened after he took you home?"

Charlie banged his head against the dashboard. His memories were like puzzle pieces, not making the right fit. "I want to believe you. I'm not questioning your judgment. But something happened at that meeting. The sheriff is lying his butt off. He said I was doing drugs in the park. Then he took me to the hospital. I never went to the hotel."

"You don't strike me as a Pot Head. But if you did light one up in the park. It would've been after the sheriff dropped you off. I saw the cruiser leave The Source compound. That's for certain."

"I feel like the sheriff is playing mind games with me. Everything I say he contradicts. It's like I'm taking crazy pills when I'm around him."

"That's what the sheriff does. Welcome to my world. Don't be fooled by the plastic smile and the happy talk."

"I have a vague image of a girl embedded in my mind."

Katie slapped Charlie on the arm. "Look at you, tiger. Got a girlfriend already in Boonville."

"Not like that. A girl was at the meeting, her face familiar. A name is on the tip of my tongue. One of the kids I lost."

The Honda idled in front of the hospital. Katie turned the radio all the way off. "Excuse me. Wait a minute. What kids?"

"This is going to sound stupid. Like I'm a Pot Head. I came up here with a group of teens. After the crash, the twelve teens disappeared. Am I taking crazy pills? Saying it out loud makes me feel loony."

Katie slapped her knee. "Charlie Tanner. That's the dumbest thing I've ever heard. Kid's don't vanish in thin air," she said, pretending to smoke a cigarette.

"Thank you, Captain Obvious. I blacked out and woke up with a wrecked van and missing kids. That's all I remember. Imagine having to tell twelve families I lost their kid's on the way to camp. And one of the kids joined a cult. Everything is fine."

"I'm sorry, I kid. Anything is possible, I guess. Maybe the kids walked away from the accident to get help? They scattered around Boonville, and that girl wandered into a Source meeting. They might be crazy, but they love new converts."

"Sure, why not? I've played every scenario in my head. How long was I knocked out? If they went and got help, why didn't they come back for me? Is someone searching for them? Did aliens capture them? After the crash, something got knocked loose in my brain. The whole thing makes no sense. You think I'm a Pot Head, don't you?"

Katie smiled. "I'm sure the accident is true. The missing kids are a hard one. But, hey, what do I know? I've been drinking the Kool-Aid of a religious cult for six years. I'm not exactly a reliable source for not believing in weird stuff. Maybe the missing kids part isn't true? The crash scrambled your brain. And you never took those kids to camp? Possible?"

"You sound a lot like the sheriff. Always questioning my memory. I guess that's how cults work. How do I know you're not working together? You run in the same cult circles. Nothing in this town has made me want to trust anyone or anything. How did you find me here? Did the sheriff call you?"

"Well, yeah. What does that have to do with anything?"

"Oh, I don't know. You see me leave the meeting. But don't think to check on me? You come and pick me up at the hospital, pretending to not know where I am. Sounds fishy to me."

"Yeah, you're right, Charlie. You have no reason to believe me. For all you know, the sheriff and I are crafting a master plan to ruin your life. But what's to say I'm not working *against* him? Why risk my life to help you? That doesn't sound like someone trying to ruin your life. But you don't have to listen to me. You're a big boy. Come to your own conclusions."

Charlie paused for a beat. "Why are you *really* here? Why help me?"

"The sheriff called and told me to pick you up. He set up the room at the Boonville Hotel, too. I've learned you don't question the boss. If I do what he says, I have leverage. He thinks nothing of it. If he suspects someone is going against his authority, watch out. I don't know why I'm here. But I've always believed you do the right thing, even if it makes little sense."

Charlie wanted to believe every word. Nothing so far made him worry about Katie and her integrity. She was one of the most genuine people he'd ever met. Yet his foggy brain was making him paranoid.

"Nothing makes sense. And nothing is normal, I get it. But let's prove myself wrong. I want to go back to The Source. Maybe if I revisit the area, my memory will return. I need to find that girl. If I find her, I think it will unlock some of these mysteries."

Katie said, "Brilliant plan. Let's do it. I'll take you to The Source compound. We'll go tonight. But I don't want to be seen. You're on your own again."

The enthusiasm of Katie surprised Charlie. She was trying to help despite his growing paranoia.

"I know it will probably be a dead end. But thanks for seeing this through."

"No problem, Pot Head."

Charlie called his dad one more time.

Nothing.

Chapter Ten

Later that night, Katie picked up Charlie in front of the Boonville Hotel. Charlie had taken another nap and could've slept for days. He stood on the curb waiting for Katie and called his mom with no answer. Charlie was defeated as his folks were MIA.

Katie leaned across the Honda to the passenger window. "What's up, cult hunter?"

Charlie opened the door and plopped into the front seat. Pet Sounds was playing. "Cult hunter? What is that supposed to mean?"

"I made it up. You know, like following in your dad's footsteps."

"I don't think so. I've seen enough of the cult world to engage in other pursuits. And, apparently, my folks disavowed me. Nobody will call me back. I'm hoping Dad shows up in the morning. Not looking forward to the awkward conversation, 'Hey, dad. I crashed the church van. And all the kids are gone. Please visit me in prison.'"

"Nobody's going to prison. We'll figure all this out. Tonight is the first step in the right direction. We find that girl, and things start making sense. A logical explanation will emerge, and we'll get you home unscathed. Did you notice the music?"

Charlie appreciated the positivity of Katie despite her blunt exterior. She was a well-adjusted person for being part of a cult. "I noticed the tunes. Is that an 'I'm sorry' music choice because of earlier today?"

"Sorry? I don't think I was in the wrong. You were the one with all the accusations."

"Good point. Sorry about that. My brain is a fog of contradictions, and my body feels like it was in a crash. Oh, wait, it was... I think," Charlie said, with a smile, "I just want to go home. I never wanted to be here. Please accept my apology."

"Accepted."

Katie drove in her typical reckless style out to The Source compound. Charlie said little and enjoyed the darkness. Only Pet Sounds played softly in the background. "Wouldn't It Be Nice," echoed through the quiet of the Boonville countryside. Charlie thought, *Wouldn't it be nice if I'd never said yes to being the pastoral assistant. None of this would have happened.* But Katie was the silver lining.

"What ya thinking about?" Katie asked, breaking the silence.

"Nothing. Missing home. Enjoying the soothing sounds of the Beach Boys. Wishing I was at the ocean."

"Can't help you with an ocean in the middle of Missouri. But how about a cult compound?"

Katie slowed the Honda as she neared the wrought-iron fence of The Source compound. She turned off the radio. "No time for reflection. We're here. I'll hit the lights and drop you before the meeting space. You can walk the rest of the way."

Charlie gazed out the window of the Honda. The fence

brought back a hint of a memory. "Did we come here last night? Was it night?"

"Yes."

"The fence looks familiar. Not sure if that matters. But it's something."

"I'm no expert in memory recall. But, get out, walk around. The building will be unlocked, and nobody will be around. We don't trust in locks; we walk by faith. It's safe out here. Today is Thursday, which means most of the community will be up the hill. Just don't make a ruckus, and you'll be fine."

"Sheesh. That's a lot to remember for someone with a broken brain. If I get caught, I'll tell them Katie sent me."

"Please don't. If you get in a pinch. Text or call. I'll come rescue you."

Katie slowed the Honda about fifty yards from the meeting building and cut the lights. "Here's your stop. I'll hang out up the road. When you're done, text, and I'll come for you."

Charlie opened the door. He leaned back into the car. "Thanks for this. Not sure what I'm doing. But I need to do something. Moving ahead is better than standing still."

"Truth, my friend. Godspeed."

Charlie limped toward the meeting building. He heard the crunch of the gravel under his sneakers. The compound was eery with little movement on the grounds. A nylon sign hung above the entrance of the meeting building. The sign triggered something and flooded pieces of a memory into Charlie's mind.

He strolled across the porch area of the building, glancing inside a bank of windows—no signs of life. A board creaked under his foot, causing his heart to leap. He scanned the area, realizing he made the sound. Charlie reached for the door. No locks. The metal double door yawned open.

Charlie stood in the middle of the dark meeting space. A guitar and drum kit sat on a small stage in the back of the room.

Another memory flooded Charlie's brain. Something about music. In the corner were a coffee maker and an empty plate. An image of a cookie caused Charlie to smile and realized he was hungry.

Charlie wasn't sure how the brain recalled memories. He wasn't sure why he needed to prove the sheriff wrong. But being in the meeting space was important, and it was working. The room was feeling like a familiar place. He could almost recreate the night. Not with fine details. But at least the main plot of the movie.

One scene, a man, standing on the stage, and another staring him down. Red eyes blaring through the center of his chest. A second scene, music, and food. A third, the sheriff. The movie in no particular order but the scenes forming the whole of the story. Bits and pieces and no wholes. But enough to know the sheriff is a liar.

Charlie paced the space and allowed whatever other memories for the movie to flood his mind as needed. He circled the space and the most important scene and plot point, the mystery girl. Like she was standing next to him. He paused and tried to let an image, name, anything come into the far off places of his brain.

The young girl had brown hair—about sixteen. Charlie could hear her laugh. Not laughter from the night of the meeting. Some other time and place and in another location. In a church van. The back of a church van. Charlie held his temples, thinking it would help him focus.

The memories from the night before finally clicking in. He saw the girl in vivid color: brown hair, sixteen, and a sweet smile. Charlie was searching for a name. The name on the tip of his tongue because the girl was undoubtedly from the church group.

Flash of lighting in Charlie's brain. Lindsey Sparks.

Charlie felt a sense of euphoria come over his body. All the confusions and lying of the sheriff were proving to be wrong. He wanted to trust his own mind and what had transpired in the last couple of days. He was scared and confused about why his parents weren't answering the phone. But the image of the girl was a reminder Charlie wasn't living in an alternative universe. The world the sheriff was trying to create in Charlie's mind. What did all of it mean precisely? No idea. Like Katie said, first steps.

Charlie opened the door, inhaled the warm evening air, and stood on the porch. He texted Katie that he was ready to leave the compound. With the image of the girl, it was enough motivation to keep going. *First steps.* It encouraged him that Lindsey was okay, and maybe the rest of the group were nearby. A rational explanation for their disappearance not far behind. Why Lindsey was at The Source, another riddle to solve. But Charlie was excited to tell Katie and figure out the next steps.

Charlie waited for Katie on a chair on the porch of the meeting space. He tapped his feet on the porch with the growing fullness of a bladder. Charlie needed to take a leak. He jumped off the porch to the side of the meeting building. Charlie walked along the side of the building and found another building behind the space. A large shed which held lawn equipment and other supplies. The shed door was half-open.

Charlie did his business on the side of the shed. The open shed door intrigued him. He walked inside and turned on his cell phone light—the light trained on a wall of clippers, tools, and shelves of gas and oil. Charlie noticed two tractors and a car.

A vehicle covered by a blue tarp sat in the corner. The tarp was falling off, and Charlie wanted to get a better look. A classic car, maybe a 64 or 65 Ford Falcon convertible. Charlie had a crush on this era of the vehicle. Reminded him of the beach.

He removed the tarp to see inside.

A girl slouched in the passenger seat.

Lindsey Sparks.

Dead.

Chapter Eleven

Charlie texted Katie a second time. "Come fast. Meet you at the road."

He limped out of the shed and met the Honda down the gravel road. Charlie's ankle was killing him after a hundred-yard jog to meet Katie. After finding the dead girl, the adrenaline helped keep the pain at bay, but not all the way.

"I found the girl," Charlie said, huffing and puffing, as he leaned on the hood of the car.

"You found the girl in your mind? Or you found her, found her?"

Charlie gasped for air. "She's dead."

"Ha, ha. It's late. I don't have time for games."

Katie watched Charlie wipe sweat from his forehead. She noticed his eye puffing up with tears. This was no joke. "I'm done with this town. She's dead. Her name is Lindsey Sparks. A girl in our youth group."

Katie let the weight of the statement settle for a beat. "Are you sure it's the girl from your youth group? You're sure she's dead?"

"I'm certain it's Lindsey. I found her body in a shed behind the meeting space. I'm no doctor. But she was white as a ghost and not moving."

"Let's see her. Maybe she's part of our community. Not one of your kids."

"My mind is a mess. But I'm 99% certain. It's Lindsey."

Katie refused and wanted to examine the dead body. "Get in the car, and we'll check it out. Let's make sure before we figure out the next steps."

Katie drove the Honda up the gravel drive to the meeting space. She scanned the compound yard to ensure nobody was watching. She was still fearful of getting in trouble for being around while on hiatus.

Charlie led Katie to the rear of the meeting space, opened the shed door, and Katie peeked into the Ford Falcon. Charlie didn't want to see the dead girl again.

"How did you end up in the shed?" Katie asked.

"I had to pee. Saw the door opened and peeked inside. Found the girl in the car."

"Got it," Katie said, leaning in closer to the body. Charlie stayed on the opposite side of the shed. "I'm not an expert either, but that girl is dead. You smell that? Her body is stinky," Katie said, leaning in closer. Charlie watched from the other side of the shed, getting sick watching Katie get so close to the dead girl. "She doesn't look familiar. Not part of our community."

"How did this happen? This makes little sense. She's one of my youth group girls. She comes to The Source, and they kill her. Why is she here? Tell me why, Katie?"

Katie shrugged. "Our community is full of weird beliefs and contradictions. But they aren't the murdering type. Intimidation and control, yes. Murder, no."

"That's nice and all. But control and intimidation are

usually a recipe for something worse. You're part of The Source. Someone gets killed. What am I supposed to think? Are you behind this?"

"Charlie, not again. I'm not the enemy. I've been on hiatus for months, not in the loop. Right now, all I do is work, eat, and sleep. If The Source is behind this, it's really disappointing."

"I'll take your word for it. But one person I don't trust is the sheriff. In my little mind exercise, it was clear the sheriff was here last night. I don't know what he said, but he stared into my soul. It was kind of freaky."

"I've seen the face. Creepy," Katie said.

"We have to pay him a visit."

Katie held up her hands and pressed them on Charlie's shoulders. "You want answers, I get it. We have a murder on our hands. But things like this are handled differently in Boonville. The sheriff, like I said before, doesn't like accountability or being questioned. You don't just waltz into his office and accuse him of murder."

"Katie, you have drunk the Kool-Aid in epic proportions. This is murder. I don't care if you live in Boonville or on Mars. Murder is murder. You call the police. It's time to stop playing games with these monsters. How are The Source people going to explain a dead girl on their property? Time to hold the sheriff to account."

Katie and Charlie left the shed and closed the door. Charlie dialed his phone as he stepped in front of the shed. A light trained in his eyes. He glanced up and blocked the light with his hand. A man came out from the shadows.

"Fine seeing you two here. What a beautiful evening in paradise."

Sheriff Brown stood between the shed and the meeting space. He slotted his black flashlight into a holster, stalked the area meandering, and spit a wad of tobacco in the grass.

Charlie pointed a finger at the sheriff. "Did you come for the girl? Cover your tracks?"

"What girl?"

"The girl you killed. Go check the shed. Not a good look for the so-called Happy Town. I can see the headline now. Youth group visits a small town in Missouri. Girl gets killed by underground cult."

The sheriff glided through the grass, unmoved by the accusations of Charlie. He spit out brown liquid and then smiled. He gave a little chuckle. "Charlie Tanner, you've been a problem since the word go. Remember when I rescued you from the park and brought you to the hospital? I told you before. I give and give, and you take and take. We give you chance after chance, and this is the thanks I get. You accuse me and our fine community of murder? That doesn't seem consistent for a preacher's kid. A man of faith, like yourself. Why do you want to hurt us despite all the things we've done for you?"

"I'm not sure what brand of faith you're dealing. But it makes me think of a band I liked from the 90s called the Spin Doctors. I didn't understand what that meant as a kid. But I now get what spin is. And you're the King of Spin. You have blood on your hands. What do you have to say about the murder of Lindsey Sparks?"

The sheriff moved toward the shed and peeked inside. He came back after about thirty seconds. He crossed himself and gazed to the dark sky. "Yes, it appears this poor girl is no longer with us. Hope she was right with the Lord. Did you know her?"

"Yes, I did. She was in my youth group. And I hope you're right with the Lord. May he have mercy on you for all the lives you've ruined."

"Mr. Tanner. You're not accusing me of murder, are you? That wouldn't be prudent."

"Yes, I am. You were here last night at The Source meeting.

Lindsey was at the meeting, too. Seems like something you'd do. What do you say to that?"

"I'd say be careful of accusing someone of murder. Especially someone who has helped you in so many ways. I find it interesting that you and Katie are here. Would you like to explain yourself?"

Katie jumped into the conversation. "You're a liar, sheriff. Charlie wasn't doing drugs in the park. I saw you take him away after the meeting. You took him to the hospital. Stop trying to create an alternative universe in his mind."

"You seem to know a lot about nothing, Ms. Katie. Why don't you listen to orders and mind your own business? Careful of what you speak. Your friend here has a drug problem. I took him to the hospital after he passed out in the park. I'm sure he's made it appear that he's a good kid. But like his father, they don't practice what they preach."

"There you go again. Telling lies. I saw your cruiser leave the compound. How do you explain that?" Katie asked, hands on her waist.

"How would you know? Were you here last night?" the sheriff asked.

"Yeah, I was. I dropped off Charlie."

"Naughty girl. You're supposed to be on hiatus. I must report you to Zebediah."

"I don't care. We're going to report you for murder. Like we always learned at The Source, light always exposes darkness. Your day will come."

The sheriff chuckled and gave a spit of chew on the ground. "I'm the law of the land. Not sure whom you're going to tell."

"We'll find a way," Charlie said.

The sheriff reached for a pair of handcuffs on his belt loop. Then a plastic zip tie. "I wasn't planning on using these tonight. But I'm going to arrest both of you. A dead girl in a shed with two potential suspects. You have the right to remain silent... it doesn't matter. I'm the law. Let's take a ride to the station. We'll chat some more."

"What? We had nothing to do with this, and you know it. Take these handcuffs off," Charlie said, squirming his wrists from the grip of the sheriff.

Katie whispered to Charlie. "It's not worth it. Don't make it worse."

The sheriff tossed them into his cruiser and they headed to the Boonville Police Department.

Chapter Twelve

Jim and June Tanner strolled the streets of their suburban neighborhood outside Kansas City. June held a leashed labradoodle in one hand that galloped along. She held her husband's hand in the other as the couple chatted about the weather and their kids' future.

Jim said, "I haven't heard from Charlie yet. I'm regretting sending him to camp with those kids. Too much responsibility, too soon."

"He'll be fine, honey."

"You're right. But he doesn't want to follow in my footsteps. I've always romanticized seeing your oldest son become part of the family business. His grandfather was a preacher, I'm a preacher, why not continue the legacy?"

June forced a half-smile and then yanked the dog from walking in the neighbor's flowers. "You know how I feel about it. Let your kids try different things and see what sticks. Charlie has always been the creative one. Writing all those stories and playing music with his band. He's not the preacher type. God's given him unique gifts, and that's perfectly fine."

"You're always the wise one. I just hope everything's going okay. Charlie can be a scatterbrain."

"Charlie has his moments. But he's a responsible kid. Aren't you going up to Boonville tomorrow, anyway? Give him some space—kids need to fail if they're going to learn anything valuable. Our generation thinks ninth place trophies are helping our kids navigate real life. I think they're becoming soft."

"June... that isn't like you. You sound like me. You're right. I'll stop worrying," Jim said, checking his phone for texts.

June leaned down to scoop up poop from the dog. She tossed it into a neighbor's trash receptacle. "You spend so many years picking up your kid's poop, literally and metaphorically," June said, looking at Jim for a response, "And then you blink, and they're all grown up and out on their own. Charlie's a unique kid and will figure out his God-given path. All our kids will be fine. If they can survive a pastor's home, they can survive anything life throws at them. Speaking of work. How's the other job going in Boonville?"

Jim shook his head. "Not good. What a sad situation. Two steps forward and two steps back. We rescued this girl from The Source, got her counseling and a new home. But the local authorities are giving us the runaround. I'm going down there to meet with a local agent on the ground. Hoping to find options for getting these loonies shut down."

June smiled. "Would you run the agency full time if you could? I see that twinkle in your eye."

Jim nodded. "It's rewarding work. The challenge is finding the financial resources to justify the work you're doing. A cult abuse counseling and prevention center is so niche, people don't want to touch it. It's not purely a nonprofit, and it doesn't fit nicely into the ministry category. But it's the most interesting and challenging work I do. Church work pays the bills, but the center fuels my soul."

Jim had built the cult abuse center on the side for many years, and it hadn't gotten to a place of financial stability yet. Secretly Jim wanted Charlie to consider joining him in taking the center to the next level. It needed some young blood, and Charlie could help be a new face for the center. With Charlie's creative gifts, Jim thought he could help with marketing. Deep down, Jim understood the pastoral assistant job wasn't Charlie's passion. But hoped that exposing him to the side hustle would open his eyes to a career possibility.

"Just be careful. Those cult people aren't all that stable," June said.

"Have you been around church people? I'll be fine."

Jim powered down his phone and restarted it.

June slapped his arm as they turned a corner in the neighborhood. The dog's tongue hung to the right as he was getting overheated. "I see what you're doing. Leave Charlie alone. Let's head back, Calvin is thirsty."

"I guess when you're married for twenty-five years, you read each other's minds. And phone habits."

"Yes, dear. I understand. You're waiting for Charlie to call or text. Besides, he only calls when in trouble. He's fine."

Jim stalled in the middle of the street. He stood akimbo. "Wow, honey. That was something special. You read my mind. You should work at the center."

"No, thank you. Keeping you in line is a full-time job."

"Sorry for being a nervous nelly. I just sent my eighteen-year-old kid on the youth church camp trip. Charlie is my responsibility as one of our staff. I just want these thirteen souls to be safe, that's all."

June ripped the phone from Jim's hand. She scrolled the texts and recent calls. "Told you, nothing. Just like the last ten times you checked. Charlie will call when he calls. If he gets in trouble, he'll figure it out. He's a lot more responsible than you were at his age. When I met you at eighteen, you certainly weren't taking kids to youth camp. You were drinking beer with your buddies behind the barn."

"True."

June dropped Jim's phone in her sweatshirt pocket. "I'm going to hold on to this until the walk is over. You're on phone restriction."

"Fine."

Jim and June finished the walk. June took Calvin to the backyard for water. Jim told June he was going to check on a sprinkler in the front yard. June disappeared out of view.

Jim made sure June had left into the back. He pulled out a second phone hiding in his jacket pocket and dialed. "Hey, Rick, it's Jim. How are things on the ground? Anything I need to know?"

The man on the other line said, "I'm undercover checking out the compound. Let you know what I find."

"You see my kid yet? I'm getting a little worried. He was supposed to arrive at lunch. And it's late afternoon. I'm coming up tomorrow, but let me know."

"No signs of him yet. I'll ask around."

Jim powered down the phone and jammed it into his waistband under his jacket.

Chapter Thirteen

Sheriff Brown stalked Katie and Charlie in a six-by-six cell in the bowels of the police station. He paced back and forth in front of the bars. He dragged his nightstick along the bars. Clank. Clank. Clank. The kids held their heads in their hands. Exhausted from the emotional toll after finding the dead girl.

"It didn't have to be this way," the sheriff said, brushing the bars of the cell with his stick.

"You didn't have to be a monster either. This is a joke. That girl was already dead, and you know it. Aren't you innocent until proven guilty? I think you have it reversed," Charlie said, with bloodshot eyes.

"Not in my town. Not when visitors come into our Happy city and try to ruin the decency and freedoms we have here. I think the blood is on your hands."

Katie stayed silent.

"It's unfortunate Missouri is a death penalty state. If this goes to trial with a jury of your peers, and they find you guilty, lights out. I hope you're right with the Lord."

Katie leapt from the bench in the cell. She gripped the bars. "Go to hell. Don't think for a second you're getting away with this. That girl was with Charlie and his group. Murder goes against everything we hold dear at The Source. We are a lot of things, but not murderers. And if that's what we are. You'll make my decision after hiatus easy."

The sheriff gave a plastic smile. "I'd sit down if you know what's good for you. These allegations are assuming a lot. I'm no murderer. I protect the innocent. The Source is a beacon of light in Boonville, Missouri, and the world. But maybe the girl on hiatus is rubbing shoulders with too much darkness. Living it up and enjoying all the world has to offer. Blinding you to the Truth. I'm sure Charlie isn't helping. Has he offered you drugs yet?"

Katie took a swipe at the sheriff through the bars. Charlie watched in amusement and enjoyed the feistiness of Katie. He also appreciated someone standing up for him in front of the sheriff. From the first moment of arriving in Boonville, the sheriff hasn't liked Charlie for any reason.

Charlie, in a moment of weakness, wondered if he could've murdered Lindsey. Maybe in the blackout, he took her out. His mind was constantly going in and out of clarity. He wondered what was reality and what was a dream? The lines blurred of truth and lies. But he wouldn't let the sheriff win the battle of his mind.

Charlie shot back, "Don't start that again. You know I didn't do drugs in the park. You know everything you say is dripping with lies. Not buying it. If anyone has blood on their hands, it's you."

Charlie surprised himself with the boldness he displayed toward the sheriff. He was not one for engaging in confrontation. It was one reason he didn't stand up to his dad and tell him the idea of being a pastor wasn't his heart's desire.

The sheriff ramped up his tapping of the nightstick against the cell bars. No longer taps, now slams of aggression. "Charlie Tanner, tough guy. I like this side of you. I see a lot of your dad inside you. The coward that thinks destroying the lives of innocent people is a sport. Does Jim believe making money off the lives of innocent people is right? Doesn't seem like the righteousness he preaches about on Sundays?"

"Don't bring my dad into this. My dad has done nothing wrong with the counseling center. He only intervenes when the law is broken or people are abused. He's not making money off innocent people and only helping the hurting. And by the looks of this town. He has his hands full."

"Why don't you ask your friend what it's really like?" the sheriff said, glaring at Katie, sitting on the bench in the corner of the cell.

"Leave me out of this," Katie said

"Is that because you're on hiatus? Sowing your wild oats out in the world? No desire for protecting Truth. You know, I've never liked that doctrine of The Source. It gives weak-willed people an out. What happened to people dedicating themselves to something in life or death? Sacrificing themselves for a greater cause. I fought in the first Gulf War. The guys I fought with would never take a year's vacation to figure things out."

"Hiatus has been great. I don't have to hang around guys like you every day. I forgot how kind the world can be sometimes."

"Careful what you wish for. Doesn't the Proverbs say what appears to lead to life, leads to death? Careful, or you'll be joining Mr. Tanner in the gas chamber. I think being an accomplice to murder is liable to the death penalty, too,"

"Believe your own myths all you want. I go to sleep

knowing the truth. We've done nothing wrong. I wonder how you sleep at all?" Katie said.

"I sleep well by serving a greater cause. I take care of the people of this town and give our community everything I have. Unlike some who take breaks to find themselves. No breaks for the weary. I hope you find what you're looking for."

Charlie cut him off. "Leave her alone. So what's the plan? Do we get a call or something? Or do we rot in this cell for the rest of our lives?"

"No more calls. Be a man and defend yourself. The stories you tell don't add up. Wasn't your dad supposed to come and meet you a couple days ago? Not surprising that he was a no-show. Sounds like something that a snake would do. Or you're lying, which is likely."

Charlie was doing everything possible to not totally blow a casket. "Stop it. Why would I lie about such a thing? You're the liar. I've already called them. They'll come. My dad's a pastor. Emergencies happen at the church all the time: sick people, death, committee meetings. There's a reason. But what I'd like to know is where the rest of my group are? You already killed Lindsey. How about the other eleven? Are they safe?"

The sheriff found a chair across from the cell and settled into the cushioned chair. He sighed. "People don't vanish, Mr. Tanner. How many times must we go over this? If you brought a group to our Happy town for some unexplained reason, we'll find them. They'll be safe. Remember, I protect the innocent. "

"Where's my van? Can I see it? I'm ready to go home now," Charlie said, glancing back to Katie, laying down on the bench in the cell.

"It's still at Bob's Garage. Not drivable. It was a mess when you brought it in. They're ordering parts. It will take a few more days. And who said you can leave? I tell you when you leave."

"Give me another car. A rental."

"Take that up with Bob. Not my problem," the sheriff said, now agitated.

"Let us out of here. Or I'm calling our family lawyer."

A man in the Tanner's church was a lawyer. William Story helped Jim with his church affairs and his counseling center.

"I decide what happens in this department and what happens in my town. We'll investigate the dead girl and get back with you."

A phone on the wall above the sheriff rang. He reached above his head and picked up the phone. The sheriff spoke in hushed tones and then placed the phone gently back on the receiver.

He rose from the chair, wrangled his keys, and headed to the cell. He then unlocked the cell. "The angels must've shone on you tonight. You can go. I'll have someone get your car," he said, staring at Katie.

Charlie and Katie glanced at one another in confusion. But wanted to leave before the sheriff changed his mind. *Who was on the phone?*

Before they left Boonville PD, the sheriff called out, "Count your lucky stars tonight. We'll meet again."

Chapter Fourteen

Katie cranked up Old Town Road in the Honda as they sat in the empty Boonville PD parking lot. She screamed at the top of her lungs. Katie banged her head on the steering wheel. She fought back tears from the intense moments in the jail cell. She punched Charlie in the arm.

"Try screaming; it helps."

Charlie gave a sideways smile and joined in the fun. He screamed and banged his hand against the passenger door. It worked. The stress of the last couple of days melted away. Charlie wondered if screaming and yelling were more fruitful than counseling? Maybe his dad could work it into his practice?

Katie turned off the radio. "I'm better, you?"

"Much."

"I've never seen the sheriff like that. Sheriff Brown is a handful and can rub the wrong way. But something in his voice was different tonight. He's trying to pin the murder on us. What are we going to do?" Katie asked.

"Boonville is a circus, and Brown is the ringleader. I just

want to go home. Can you talk to someone? How about your folks?"

"No way. They're on the inside. The allegiance to The Source is too strong. They won't believe anything I say. Besides, I'm on hiatus. We're not exactly on good terms. I've hinted that I might leave. A lot of family drama right now."

"I have to find my Dad. Lindsey Sparks is dead. The rest of the group might be, too. Not sure what I'm supposed to do about that? Dad will."

Katie turned off the car. She removed the keys and handed them to Charlie. "You find your dad. Take my car. If anyone finds out about this, I'm in deep trouble. Most likely will seal my fate about staying with The Source. But after what I witnessed in the jail, we *need* backup."

Charlie examined the keys like they had two heads. "Come on, Katie. I feel weird about leaving you, leaving the kids. I don't want the sheriff to do anything to you."

"Everything is a risk. But we walk by faith, not sight, right?"

"I guess. But I don't want you to get hurt."

Katie leaned in, and Charlie backed up. She moved in again and kissed his cheek. "I like you, Charlie. You have a great heart deep inside that Beach Boy loving frame. Take the car and find your dad. We'll figure it out. But please do me one favor. Come back. I don't want to fight alone."

Charlie nodded.

The kiss from Katie gave Charlie renewed energy. Not that he was 100% comfortable leaving Boonville. Which sounded bizarre considering all the things going down in the town. But his dad had research and intelligence on The Source and thought he could make something happen. He was connected to local authorities, had a lawyer, and could help with the Lindsey Sparks predicament.

"Thanks for this kiss. That was nice. I like you too, you

crazy cult loving chick. I wish you lived in Kansas City, and we didn't have to meet under these bizarre circumstances. I'll take care of the Honda and come right back with my dad. Everything will be fine."

Katie yanked out a small wallet. She opened it and handed Charlie a wad of cash. "I don't have much, but here's some gas and snack money. Road trip essentials."

Charlie held the wad of cash. "Thanks. I'm a little strapped on cash. I lost my wallet after the crash."

"Before you leave, can you take me back to the hotel? I have a shift in an hour. And I don't have a car," Katie said with a wink.

Charlie drove to the hotel and dropped off Katie. He grabbed his bag from the room and thanked Katie again, and promised to come back soon.

The Honda drove down Main Street, away from the Missouri River. Charlie headed right down a two-lane highway, which headed out of town. The sun set, and darkness fell across Missouri. He cranked up Pet Sounds, *God Only Knows*, and sang at the top of his lungs. Something in the drive was building a sense of anticipation. All the pain of the last couple of days fading for a minute. The warmth of the summer air coming through the window. Music. A closeness growing between Katie and himself.

The accident and the pain in Charlie's body finding relief masked by the hum of road noise. The mystery of losing the kids, wondering if they were okay, or sad, or alone? All paused. The hatred growing over Sheriff Brown faded.

Charlie, lost in thought, examined a sign for Boonville passing on the left.

Boonville: Happiness is Our Last Name

. . .

A wooden sign with the Boonville motto had a white family hugging each other in the corner. Like something from a 50s magazine ad selling insurance. It made Charlie giggle. Boonville nothing like the idyllic imagery of the sign.

Charlie slapped his knee and sang some more Beach Boys tunes. Getting lost in the music, he didn't notice the curve in the two-lane highway. Something in the highway's curve triggered a memory. Was it the location of the crash? Maybe. The site of the crash was a few miles outside of town.

Charlie kept singing, and the ninety-minute ride to Kansas City would be a breeze. He couldn't wait to see his family. *There's a rational explanation of why they haven't called, right? Church emergency. Busy. The world is full of mystery. But most things have a rational explanation.*

Charlie glanced to the right. A Boonville sign appeared:

Boonville: Happiness is our Last Name

What the heck? How many signs does this place have? I just saw the sign leaving town. Why another? Charlie rubbed his eyes. *Was I falling asleep?*

Charlie hit another curve as the lights shone on a guardrail. Another memory of the crash burst into his brain. Chatting kids, farts, Charlie yelling in the back. Darkness.

Something didn't settle right in his stomach. *What is going on?*

Charlie saw more light up ahead. He rubbed his eyes to see the upcoming lights.

It was the lights of Boonville. *Come on. Did I turn around?*

My brain is foggy, but I'd remember if I turned around. Is that Boonville or another small town? It's dark, possible.

Charlie entered the start of Main Street. The street lined with restaurants, stores, and a bank which looked familiar. The Boonville Police Department and Boonville Hotel passed the window of the Honda.

What the heck? I'm losing my mind.

Charlie yanked the car into a parking spot in front of an ice cream shop.

Everything was closed on Main Street.

Charlie stood on the sidewalk and stared at the signs of the stores. The warm breeze of early summer pushed his blonde hair to the side.

What is going on? I'm not supposed to be here. I'm supposed to be heading east toward Kansas City. Why am I back in Boonville?

A young man about sixteen wandered up the sidewalk in front of the ice cream parlor. Charlie said, "Hey, buddy. I'm kind of lost. Are we in Boonville, Missouri?"

He smiled. "Yeah, best town in America. Happiness is Our Last Name," he said, sounding like a monotone robot, like one of those cashiers at Chick Fil-a.

"You sure?"

The young kid laughed. "Yes, sir. I've lived in Boonville my whole life. Best town..."

The street light hit the side of his face at just the right angle. Charlie noticed a cross hanging from the kid's neck. A flood of memories came into his mind. The van. Kid's laughing. The young man was in the van. *He was in that van. Why didn't he recognize me?*

"Do you remember me? My name is Charlie Tanner. You were in my van. I took you to camp. We had an accident. Please say something."

He batted his brown eyelashes. “I’m sorry, sir. I don’t know you. My name is Ryan Burden. I’m from Boonville. Can I help you get somewhere?”

Charlie told the kid to wait. He wanted to run and get Katie up the street. Charlie didn’t know what to do. He ran to the kid and started up the street but didn’t want to leave him. Charlie walked back and forth twice.

“Stay here. I need to get someone. Please...”

“I need to get going, sir. I don’t mean to be rude. But I don’t know you, and I need to get home.”

Charlie lost his cool and grabbed the shirt of the kid. “Please, I need your help. The kids are gone. I know you. What happened at the crash? Where is home?”

The kid ripped free from Charlie. He ran down the street, glancing back once, and then over a bridge out of sight.

Charlie ran for him and stopped. He fell down in a heap on Main Street and cried.

The Honda was still running.

Chapter Fifteen

Charlie jumped into the Honda and drove a couple blocks to the Boonville Hotel. He parked in a front parking spot, killed the engine, and raced through the sliding doors. He yelled into the lobby, not caring if anyone heard him.

Katie glanced up from staring at her phone. Playing a game of Angry Birds. Charlie slammed into the front desk. "Katie, I found another kid."

Katie slammed the phone on the counter. "Calm down. Let's first talk about why you're here? Did the Honda crap out?"

"No, it's fine. Parked in front. I left town and then found a kid. He's from the youth group. Ryan Burden."

The words coming out of Charlie's mouth were not computing in his brain. He was on the brink of having a meltdown. Nothing seemed to make sense, and no way Katie was going to believe him.

"Why did you come back? I thought you were headed to

Kansas City to find your pops? Did you miss me?" Katie said, giving pouty lips.

"No, I mean, yeah. But that's not why I'm back. I left, and now I'm back."

"You make little sense. What brought you back?"

Charlie was about to crawl over the desk. "Katie, I'm not crazy, right? You gave me your keys, and I left for Kansas City."

"Correct."

"I'm not dreaming, right?"

"I don't think so."

"I left Boonville and entered some freaking Twilight Zone alternative universe. I drove away from Boonville in the Honda, cranked up the tunes, and ended up back here. The city won't let me leave."

"Boonville is a weird place. We all agree. But I'm having a hard time understanding what happened. You left, and now you're back. The city essentially spit you out and then brought you back. Are you sure you didn't make a wrong turn? Are you on drugs like the sheriff suggested?"

"Not, now. I'm tired. But I don't remember making any wrong turns. What the hell is going on?"

"You need a Red Bull? I have one in the back."

"No. I'm fine. I didn't make any wrong turns. Something is seriously wrong around here. I saw Ryan, too. How is that possible?"

"Ryan?"

Charlie was rambling. "From the group. He didn't recognize me. He said he's from Boonville. But he's from my group, I swear."

"If you're certain he was in your group, why didn't he recognize you?"

Charlie slapped the counter in frustration. "Who knows?

I'm freaked out, Katie. I just want to go home. Why can't I leave? I hate this place."

"We'll get you home, I promise. Let me finish my shift, and I'll take you."

Charlie paced the lobby of the hotel. "No, we need another plan. I don't want to anger whatever other dimension Boonville is operating in. My folks won't answer my calls, and I'm going to jail for the murder of twelve teens. No need for you to get in trouble."

"I will not leave you. But can you promise this kid was in your group? Your story... well, it is a little odd."

"The kids are here in Boonville. I feel it in my bones. Even the sheriff said kids don't vanish. I saw Lindsey, rest her soul, and this other kid. The rest of them are nearby."

"A rational explanation still appears to be on the table. But why can't you leave Boonville?"

"Yes, an enormous elephant in the room. A town is holding me captive. And why didn't that kid recognize me? Why did he say he's from Boonville?"

Katie nodded. "Odd, yes. Maybe the kids have dislodged brains like you?"

"Dislodged brains? Really? Is that the medical term?" Charlie said, rolling his eyes.

"Sorry. Concussion? Amnesia? Doesn't matter. What matters is you saw a kid from the group, and that gives us hope. It's something. We just need to figure out why he didn't recognize you. There's always a rational explanation, right?"

Charlie found a couch across from the massive front desk. He plopped into the leather cushions and hung his head. "Reason appears to vanish in this town. I want explanations, but I'm running out of steam. This is all a bad, bad dream. All I wanted to do this summer was make a few bucks and figure out my life. Not too much to ask, right? Now I'm caught up in a cult, witnessed a murder, and stuck in a town from the third level of hell."

Katie came out from behind the counter. She walked to Charlie and plopped into the cushions next to him. She placed her hand on his. He enjoyed the warmth of her soft hands. "I get it. Things don't make sense. But we've always believed stuff happens for a reason. I can't explain everything that happens in Boonville. Ever since we moved here, nothing has made much sense. Not all bad, but mostly confusion and pain from my perspective. All we can do right now is take each moment as it comes and see where it leads."

Charlie appreciated the comfort in Katie's voice. "Not the pep talk I was hoping for. I hoped you'd say a special prayer to your cult god, and he'd rescue me and send me home. We can all dream, right?" Charlie said.

Katie smiled. "I wish life was that easy. But one thing I learned from The Source is family is everything. You never bail on the ones you love. I'm out on a limb trying to help you. But know *this* family will never bail. Blood is always thicker than water," Katie said, lightly tapping her chest.

"Sounds good. But we still haven't solved the riddle of Boonville. Why was Lindsey Sparks murdered? Why are kids in my group ignoring me? And please explain how you can leave a place and end up where you started?"

Katie leaned into Charlie's cheek and pecked him with a kiss. "And how can a kid from the city fall for a cult girl from the country? Curious minds want to know?"

"The mystery of all mysteries," Charlie said, as his cheeks blushed. "What was that for?"

"Just to say thanks for being a good friend. Not many guys stay long when they know I'm in a..." Katie gave quotation marks with her fingers, "Cult."

Charlie's phone buzzed in his pocket. A text. The first call since he arrived in Boonville. He got excited, thinking it was his family. "Hold that thought, I have a text," Charlie said, checking the phone.

Charlie, my name is Rick Sanchez. I'm a friend of your father's. Please meet me out front.

Charlie leapt from the couch. "Someone's meeting me out front. I have to go—a friend of my dad's. Be right back. It's something, right?"

"Can I come?" Katie said, rising from the couch.

Charlie waved Katie to follow and ran through the sliding doors.

A man in a black jacket and dark shades stood in the front of the hotel. Charlie thought the shades were odd for the evening. He called the two of them down a side alley and scanned the area like someone was following them.

"My name is Agent Rick Sanchez. I work with your father. You've messed up, kid."

Charlie held up his hands. "Excuse me. Who are you? Agent what?"

"Sanchez. We have little time. The kid you chatted with near the ice cream shop. Not a good move."

"Not a good move? I'm sorry. I left Boonville, and it spits me back here. You want to talk about bad moves? This place is a walking bad move. The worst move agreeing to take a bunch of teens to church camp. Did my father tell you that part? Agent Rick..."

"Doesn't matter. We've been on the ground working here for months. Talking to that kid is going to go one of two ways. One, nothing will happen. We get lucky. Two, someone dies. I'm hoping for the first scenario."

"Death is a common theme around here. But I have no idea what the heck you're talking about. Why is someone going to die? That kid didn't know who I am. I think we're safe."

"You believe him?" Rick asked, glancing down the alley as a car drove past.

"I err on the side of giving people the benefit of the doubt. Sure, why not?"

"People lie. That kid was lying to you."

"Yes, this town is full of death, and liars too," Charlie said, leaning against the brick wall in the alley. "Can I have a second? This is a lot to take in. The last hour has become a circus in my brain."

Agent Sanchez grabbed Charlie by the shoulders and spun him toward his face. "Listen, kid. What we're dealing with is not church camp. These people are out for blood. What happened with that kid will most likely anger the mother bee in the nest. If you know what I mean?"

"No, I don't. Please explain your metaphor."

Katie burst into the conversation. "Is Zebediah going to do something?"

The agent turned to Katie and sized her up. "Of all people, you'd understand the metaphor. Things will get ugly in this town soon if word gets back to the community. We need to get out of here. I have a house up the road. Let's go."

"Who's Zebediah again?" Charlie asked.

"The leader of The Source," Katie and the agent said in tandem.

"I'll explain more at my place. They're watching us. They're always watching us."

"Is my dad coming soon?" Charlie asked.

The agent ignored the question. He ushered them into an unmarked black sedan.

They left to the outskirts of Boonville to a house near The Source compound.

Chapter Sixteen

Agent Rick Sanchez rented a house located across from The Source compound. A two-bedroom ranch that was falling apart at the seams. Peeling paint and a faded door greeted the group as they walked up the steps—no lights on outside or inside. Charlie was nervous, and Katie appeared cautious following the mystery agent.

Sanchez fumbled with his keys and opened the creaking front door. He hit a light and tossed the keys on an end table. The living space was sparse and included a worn couch, chair, TV, and table in the corner. Papers and photos hung on the walls littering the small, dirty house.

"Make yourself at home," Sanchez said.

Charlie stood near the front door, hesitant to go further into the house. "Thank you for the kind gesture. But can you please explain who you are and what we're doing? I'm all for friendly visits. But no offense, your house looks like a serial killer lives here."

"I'm a special agent specializing in cult operations. Your father's center hired me to watch The Source. We rented this house to do our work. I'm the primary agent, and other contract agents help occasionally. Money is tight for our agency, so I'm the head guy."

Charlie thought the detailed answer was sufficient and more than he asked for.

Katie scanned the walls of photos, drawings, and arrows pointing to different people. "We appreciate your Beautiful Minds hospitality. What exactly are you watching? Is The Source a threat?" Katie asked, knowing the answer depending on how you defined *threat*.

The agent removed a black windbreaker and tossed it on a bench near the door. A gun jammed in his belt. "The Source is under local and federal investigation. That's all I can say."

"The Source is an interesting place to the outsider. But I'm sure whatever you're looking for isn't warranted. They're kind of like an extended family of sorts. Mostly good people," Katie said, still observing the photos on the wall.

"You have an intimate connection to The Source, Katie Larson. We've been watching them for months. It's good you're outside it for now. Things are getting complicated on the inside."

Katie turned away from the photos, placed her hands on her hips, and tapped her sneaker on the dirty floor. "How do you know my name? And what do you mean by complicated?"

"Like I said, we've been watching The Source for months. We know everyone associated with the group. Complicated is an acceptable way of saying not everyone is legitimate on the inside."

"Nobody's perfect. Isn't this against the law or something? Stalking people," Katie asked.

"No," the agent said in a stern tone.

Sanchez wasn't one for chit chat and appeared emotionally distant.

Charlie said, "Where's my dad? He was supposed to be up here days ago. Is everything okay?"

"He's fine. Do you kids want anything to drink? I have water, milk, or coffee?"

Charlie and Katie wanted coffee. The agent wandered into the galley-style kitchen and yanked out a coffee maker from the cupboard. "You kids are too young for coffee. It will stunt your growth."

"That's a wives' tale," Charlie yelled to the kitchen.

The agent didn't respond and prepared the coffee. He poured water into the coffee machine. He grabbed three cups and brought them out to the coffee table in the living room. He then got cream, sugar, and a spoon.

"I'm not sure how you like to doctor up your coffee."

The kids sat on the couch, and the agent sat across in a simple wooden chair. He sipped his coffee and paused a beat. The steam rising into his about thirty-five-year-old face. Sanchez had a short black crew cut style hair and a solid build. "The Source are bad people. We've been investigating fraudulent and abusive activities in their ranks. Jim Tanner was made aware of these issues as he's worked with a couple abuse victims from the community. It's good you are here. You want to stay far away from these people," Sanchez said, glaring at Katie.

Charlie said, "Where's my dad? I've called him multiple times. And my mom. Do you know anything?"

The agent sipped his coffee and shrugged. "I'm hired to investigate The Source and nothing else. Jim doesn't let me into his personal affairs."

Charlie swirled the coffee with a spoon, adding another heap of sugar. He thought the response of the agent was cold. Maybe it was his personality to be a robot and not feel anything. His training didn't allow for emotional connections with victims or the people he was helping. Charlie didn't know. But the absence of his father was still worrisome.

The agent set the coffee down on the coffee table and rose from his chair. He walked to the front window in the living room. He peeked through a maroon curtain which looked like it hadn't been washed since JFK was President. "Charlie, you met a kid on Main Street, correct?"

"Yes, sir. The kid from my youth group. He pretended to not know me."

"Are you certain the kid is from your church group?"

"Cross my heart and hope to die. Why would I lie?"

The agent paced through the living room, glancing at the photos on the walls. "I'm not accusing you of lying. I'm only trying to get the facts. Boonville is a strange place. Unexplainable things have happened in my time here. Any way you could've mistaken this kid for someone else? It was dark, and I know about the accident. Hit your head, right?"

"Come on, man. No disrespect. But you sound like the crazy people from The Source. Sheriff Brown has been playing mind games the entire time I've been in Boonville. He believes nothing I say. The accident, the kids, and the dead girl. Nothing. And now you?"

"I'm sorry, just trying to do my job. We have to cover all our bases. Did you mention a dead girl? What is that about?"

"You haven't heard? A girl turned up dead after a Source meeting. The sheriff tried to blame it on Katie and me. But we think he did it. She was also part of our group. Lindsey Sparks."

The agent examined the wall of photos. "You said Lindsey Sparks?" He pointed to a smiling girl with blonde hair. Charlie turned to see the photos on the wall. "Her?" the agent said, pointing to Lindsey.

He walked a couple feet over, "Who was the kid on Main Street?"

"Ryan something. I forget his last name."

"Ryan Burden?" the agent asked.

"That's it, I think. Not good with last names."

Charlie left the couch and watched the agent examine the photos on the wall. He noticed twelve kids in a line. All about sixteen years old. The youth group kids.

His mind raced back to the crash. The laughter, farting, and kids being kids. It was like each kid was speaking to him. He pointed at the wall. "These are them. The kids I was taking to camp. Are they okay? Please tell me they're safe."

"Grab a seat, Charlie. I need to tell you something."

The already emotionally reserved agent shifted his tone and facial expression to worry. "I appreciate you giving me the heads up on Lindsey. I'm shorthanded here in Boonville and struggling to keep up with everything. A murder by The Source isn't going to make the news, unfortunately. Lucky to make it out of the compound. I must look into this."

Charlie nodded and locked on Sanchez. His heart was beating fast and encouraged by the photos on the wall. Feeling like someone finally cared.

"Ryan Burden is a problem. The reason I said earlier tonight Zebediah might stir the nest is because of what I need to tell you."

The room was silent and awkward. Katie leaned forward on the couch.

"What I'm about to say will sound strange. But please trust me."

They nodded.

"Your father gave me a special assignment. Not related to our primary work with The Source. Operation Charlie. Which was ensuring you and the kids got here safe. Your father gave me your ETA. I waited for your arrival. When you didn't arrive with the kids, I went out to look for you."

"Did you see the crash?" Charlie asked.

"Yes, and No. I came upon your van on its side. But you weren't in the van, and neither were the twelve kids."

"Good one. Seriously, what really happened? I don't remember much, but I remember the crashed van, and I remember Snake picking me up. I remember the missing kids. I didn't vanish."

"I told you. Nothing makes sense. When I found the van with no one inside, I called your dad. He sent me pictures of you and the other teens. There had to be an explanation. I'm still searching for a rational one."

"Wait a minute. You find the van flipped over. I'm not inside. The other teens are gone. This is crazy talk. Maybe we walked back to town?" Charlie said, frustrated by the whole thing.

"I know it doesn't make sense. But here's the complication. I've been working in Boonville for months. I'm undercover. I can't give up my identity because we're close to taking our suspects down. I would have done more under normal circumstances. I had to leave before someone saw me. But on the positive side, I found you, and I've seen a couple kids around town. I can't speak for all of them, but we've identified a handful. I'm sorry about Lindsey, that's new information."

Katie said, "New information? Aren't you supposed to be the professionals? How does a girl wind up dead and you don't have information?"

"Like I said, I'm shorthanded. Things slip through the cracks. I'm working mostly alone, apart from a few contractors. The Source are masters at keeping a low profile in public."

"You didn't think to call Charlie's dad after the crash? To come and get him?"

The agent took a long pause. Then a deep breath. "I

haven't had contact with Jim for a couple days. We sent an agent to find him. I'm sorry."

"You think The Source is behind this?" Charlie asked.

"Don't know. But likely. Just like they are most likely behind the disappearance of these kids. And whatever went down at the crash."

"You're both safe here tonight. I'll make up a spot in the extra bedroom."

Charlie slept on the floor.

Katie slept in the bed.

Charlie called his dad.

Voicemail.

Chapter Seventeen

Katie brushed her teeth, washed her face, and slumbered into the ten by ten-bedroom. She was thankful for the extra clothes and toiletries the agent had on hand. She wore a long tee-shirt and sweatpants. Charlie thought she looked cute and cozy.

Charlie adjusted his pillow on the floor air mattress. He slid inside a sleeping bag.

Katie slipped under the covers of the metal-framed bed. She propped her hands behind her head on the pillow, "You alright down there, kid? What you thinking about?"

Charlie sighed. "Oh, I don't know. That we live in the Twilight Zone. My parents are being held hostage by a cult. And I'm going to live the rest of my days under the thumb of said cult. Other than that, it's all good. You?"

Katie sat up against the headboard. "Let me calm your nerves. I can't explain all the weird stuff going on, like what happened after the crash. But what I know about The Source is they don't like people messing with them. We're simple people that want to live out our days the way we see fit. Yes, these practices are often bizarre and unorthodox. But when people attack these wishes. When our freedoms are threatened. And when people question the way we do things, our leaders react in, let me say, unkind ways. Your dad wasn't on their favorite people list because he questioned the way they do things. If Agent Sanchez is found out, he'll be on the same list."

"You trust Sanchez? Telling the truth about everything?" Charlie said in a whisper, not wanting him to be heard in the room across the hall.

"I don't know the arrangement he has with your father. No reason not to. What's your read on Sanchez?"

"He appears legit. But anything is possible in this town. My read is Dad is way over his head. You don't hire a special agent to work undercover unless you're drowning in your work. My dad's a preacher who counsels cult victims on the side. I think all this crap is way beyond his pay grade."

"Sure, maybe the work is too heavy for one person. But I'm sure something he saw spooked him," Katie said.

"Like what? You're the cult expert," Charlie said.

"Who knows? But something is making him nervous to call in the big guns. I'm just saying The Source may have weird beliefs and live in the country. But they have money and resources working behind the scenes 24-7 ensuring their freedoms are not messed with."

"I'm sure The Source is the life of all the cult parties. I can't think about this stuff anymore. I'm going to sleep."

Katie agreed and clicked the night light on the end table. Charlie took only a few minutes to fall asleep. His right side still sore from the accident. The thin air mattress wasn't helping.

His mind raced with the events of the last few days. Then all the colliding thoughts turned to a dream.

The church van turned on its side. A voice calling his name. *Charlie. Charlie.*

He heard it again.

I will not hurt you. Just keep your eyes closed. Everything will be fine. Trust me.

Charlie heard other voices in the distance. Unidentified adult voices. Mostly men. And voices that sounded like younger people.

We're going for a little ride. Everything will be fine.

Charlie shot up from the air mattress. He glanced at Katie, who was giving out a light snore. Charlie was sweating. *Something happened at the crash. But what?*

Chapter Eighteen

Zebediah Mulvaney stood next to a whiteboard at the end of a long table. Twelve people sat chatting and shooting the breeze before the meeting started. Zebediah hushed the talking and wrote on the board: *Sanchez*.

"What does this name mean to you?"

A man in his late forties wearing an American flag bandana smiled and glanced at the group around the table. "We used to put this hot sauce on our tacos. It was Sanchez something or another."

A weak laugh rippled around the table.

Zebediah slammed his fist against the board. The room went silent. "Is this funny to you, Bill? This name represents the enemy. An enemy of freedom. JFK said, 'The great revolution in the history of man, past, present, and future, is the revolution of those determined to be free.' When people invade our town and try to take these freedoms. We have a mandate to respond."

Bill hung his head in shame.

"Rick Sanchez is an agent hired by our favorite person, Jim

Tanner. He's sticking his nose where it doesn't belong. And I also understand the press is on our butts. Claiming we're a cult that abuses children. You can bet our friend Jim is behind this too. Our determination to be free is being threatened, and we will not stand for it."

A woman in her mid-thirties wearing a head covering spoke up. "Master Mulvaney, we trust your leadership. What do you suggest we do?"

Mulvaney wrote another name on the board: *Ryan Burden.*

"Before we make a plan. Let's play the name game one more time. What about this one?"

No answers.

Zebediah grabbed his temples and rubbed. "Call it a failure of leadership on my part. Or call it sheer incompetence. I have disturbing news. We found one of our newest recruits on Main Street walking around. Please tell me how the hell this happens?"

A cough was heard at the end of the table. A man in his sixties wearing a trucker hat tried to hide a second cough in his hand. Zebediah glided to the end of the table to meet the cougher. "Is there something you want to say?"

"No, Master Mulvaney. I'm fighting a cold. Sorry for interrupting the meeting."

Zebediah leaned over the man and tapped the bill of his hat. "Do you know anything about Ryan? Is this your doing?"

"No, sir."

Zebediah relented from harassing the man and wandered back to the whiteboard. "Sitting around this table in The Source Leadership Council. The highest order in our community. You're my key leaders—the future of The Source. And you had one job to do. Ensure our recruits aren't seen out in public before they are ready. How difficult are these instructions to follow? Please, someone, tell me," he shouted.

Silence.

"Great, the silent treatment. While Ryan Burden wanders down Main Street like he's been a resident of Boonville his entire life. We all know these foundational truths... The intake process breaks down when we allow new recruits to be out in public before their time. So, who's going to confess? Don't let the rest of the group suffer."

The leadership council looked at one another. Who is the guilty party?

A young man in his mid-twenties wearing a *Hard Rock Las Vegas* tee shirt about the middle of the table raised his hand. "I told Ryan he could go for a walk. He'd spent all day in classes and done some excellent work. I said he could go get a walk near the river. I'm sorry, Master. I had a moment of weakness."

Zebediah strolled to the man sitting at the table. All eyes were on them. The awkwardness in the room was thick like fog after a fall rain in Missouri.

He leaned into the man. Zebediah's fiery breath on the man's neck. "Oh, a moment of weakness. You're part of the leadership council. We don't have room for weakness. You thought a recruit could go for a walk because he did well in their classes? Isn't that nice? What do you think this teaches our community?"

"I'm not sure, Master."

"Let me think... Weakness. Our recruits must learn commitment and discipline. How to fight through the pain when things get hard. No walks, no easy street."

A collection of mumbles and half grumbles filled the meeting space.

"You follow orders, and the orders are to never allow a recruit to be in public until they're properly trained. You put our community at severe risk of losing everything tonight. What do you say for yourself?"

"I'm sorry... it won't happen again, Master."

"That's right, it won't happen again because you're going to have a review class in discipline and commitment. Have some of that weakness beat out of you. I think a Shaming is in order."

He picked the man up by his armpits and dragged him to the front of the room. "The only proper consequence is a good old fashioned Shaming. We haven't done one of these in a long time. I only use these as a last resort. Maybe it will remind our community of the mission and what we're fighting for."

A woman spoke up, "Master, we must vote on any Shaming according to our laws. No one person can implement a Shaming unless a majority of the leadership council agrees. Should we vote?"

A man tapping the table spoke, "With all due respect. I don't think this calls for a Shaming. Jerry wasn't trying to do any harm. He made a mistake. I don't think this is malicious."

Zebediah slammed his fist on the table. "No, I say what's malicious. Ryan Burden went walking around Boonville like a free citizen. And you know what happened? Do you want to hear the rest of the story?"

"Yes, sir."

"He ran into Charlie Tanner."

An audible gasp shot through the meeting space in the basement of The Source compound.

"Of all the people in town. Charlie Tanner is the last person we want running into a recruit. So I'm thinking a Shaming is in the highest order. Shall we vote?" Zebediah said.

The man said, "I still don't think it's a good idea. Charlie Tanner is not a threat. He's clueless. We can cover our tracks and make this go away."

"Charlie Tanner... if he's anything like his father, he'll be persistent. And besides, we don't have to vote. I can make one call and make this happen. According to our laws, the High Priest can veto any vote for Shaming. I'm going to make a call."

Zebediah yanked out a phone from his jeans and walked to the back of the room. He dialed and had a brief conversation with someone on the line. He came back to the group with a defeated look.

"Someone got lucky today. But we still can vote. Let's do it. All in favor say I, all others say neigh."

The group yelled out their votes. Seven "I's" and five "neighs."

"Fine, we don't have a majority. You don't want a Shaming. But I don't want this to happen again. I'm the majority. We're growing our community leaps and bounds. I can't have this display of incompetence on my watch. The next time, the High Priest will have a different response. He will blow up this leadership council and find loyal disciples. Be warned."

The council nodded, stood, and headed for the door.

Mulvaney yelled out, "Someone needs to find Rick Sanchez. Make sure he causes no more problems for our pursuit of freedom."

Chapter Nineteen

Rick wore dark shades and a ball cap to hide his identity. Spent most of his days in Boonville trying to avoid contact with the locals as much as possible. The only giveaway was his six-foot-five frame, which made quiet entrances difficult.

The kids joined Sanchez for morning coffee at the Boonville Java House. The only coffee shop on Main Street. Sanchez pretended to be a writer from out of town when asked by locals on his many visits to the joint. Charlie was starving, and Katie needed coffee... all the coffee.

They ordered coffees, bagels, and found a table in the back of the shop. Charlie slapped a mound of cream cheese on the bagel and threw back coffee like it was his last. "Hungry?" Sanchez asked, scanning the restaurant like a paranoid drug addict.

"Didn't sleep well," Charlie said, ripping off a piece of bagel and handing it to Katie. "Taste this."

She refused and rolled her eyes. "You're gross and have

cream cheese on the side of your mouth. Slow down, they have plenty more bagels if you need another."

Charlie smiled at Katie with bagel in his teeth.

She ignored him and focused on Sanchez.

Sanchez said to Charlie, "Was your lack of sleep because of the mattress? It's thin. I can pump it up tonight."

"No, it was fine. Bad dream," Charlie said.

"What did you dream about?" Sanchez said.

Charlie sipped the coffee and slowed down on his inhaling of the bagel. He hesitated to answer the question. Charlie was tired of every story and the thought of being questioned. "It was nothing. My dad says dreams are meaningless. I had a long day. When I'm tired, the mind goes crazy."

Katie bit into a bagel and then washed it down with a latte. "Come on, Tanner. We have nothing else to talk about. Spill the beans. Was it a dirty dream?"

"No, sicko. If it was, I'm not telling you guys."

Charlie glanced at Katie and then the agent. "Fine. Don't make fun. It was about the crash."

"What about the crash?" the agent asked.

"You won't believe me. Never mind, I'll keep it between me and God."

"Well, God isn't here. Why not tell us? It could be helpful for my work."

Charlie wiped his hands with a napkin. "Fine, whatever. There was a voice. It was calling out to me. Saying everything is going to be okay. Happy? I told you, it means nothing."

The agent perked up. "Anything else?"

"I heard voices of kids. Maybe the kids from our group. They sounded real."

The agent nodded. "I know it was a dream. But in our training at the agency, we learned dreams can be heightened because of trauma. It's like your brain takes in information even when we're not conscious of it. The mind is a complex organ but often gives us clues to the truth."

"One time, I dreamed I was a unicorn. And it turns out I have an uncle on my mom's side who is," Katie said, holding back a laugh.

Agent Rick ignored the comment.

"Anything else you can remember from the dream?"

Charlie nodded. "Yeah, it felt real. I've had lots of dreams, but not like this one. Hard to distinguish between reality and fantasy. I woke up kind of freaked out."

Sanchez wrote the details on a small notepad. "This is helpful, Charlie. We can't trust every dream, but the details are interesting. When I took your father's orders and went out to find you, like I said, you were missing, and so were the kids. I think the dream might confirm some details of what happened after the crash. Maybe these voices are the clues we need?"

"Yeah, it confirms that kids don't vanish into thin air. I'm all for interpreting dreams, Prophet Daniel. But I wouldn't bet all your money on one vague dream. Don't you need more to go on?" Katie asked.

"I'd never base a case solely on a dream. I don't have that kind of training. But like I said earlier, dreams can give us clues. Sometimes dreams are merely to confirm reality. Something happened after the crash, and we need to find out what. Did someone show up at the scene before I did?"

Charlie wrapped his hands around the paper coffee cup. "If kids don't vanish, and you and my dad have been working in the area for months, who's saying the crash wasn't planned? Someone caused the van to crash, took the kids, and then messed with my head? Something the sheriff could be down with. He hates my dad, and apparently me, too. Not sure why?"

Rick took a couple more notes. "I like how you think, kid. Nothing is off-limits. I've heard crazier ideas. Sheriff Brown is a few cards short of a full deck, from what I can tell. It seems like something he'd orchestrate. But why?"

Katie watched in amusement with the conspiracy theories flying across the table. She finished off her coffee. "I know why. The Source is always looking for new recruits. They like em' young. I don't want to believe they'd stoop this low. But maybe they had some plan to brainwash your group? They can be very persuasive—my family case in point. Hey, if you're going to listen to a dream. Why not consider my theory?"

Sanchez took down Katie's ideas. "Nothing is off the table. How do new recruits come into your organization?"

"Something of a mystery. But what I've gathered is they've set up underground communities for the sake of recruitment. My family lived in Florida and was recruited to come here. It worked."

"Do they have communities all over the country?"

"I don't know for certain. I think the goal is always to get new recruits to Boonville. They see it as The Source Mecca."

Sanchez scribbled feverishly. "This is important information. I had little on their recruiting practices. Thank you."

Katie pretended to bow in her seat. "Anything to help."

Sanchez noticed the morning was getting late. He didn't want to be in public for too long of stretches. Katie headed for a shift at the hotel, and Charlie spent the day at the rental house.

Chapter Twenty

Charlie spent the day at the house laying low. Playing a lot of games on his phone and not much else. With all that was going on, the restful day was a needed reprieve. Katie was busy for the day working and hanging out with a friend.

The next morning before sunup, Agent Rick tied up his running shoes and put on his shades and cap. The June summer weather still cool in the mornings, about seventy. Rick was tiring of the daily monotony in Boonville. But the running routine was keeping him sane.

The plan was to run around the perimeter of The Source compound and check out the area where they found Lindsey Sparks. Agent Sanchez planned to leave early before the sun was up to avoid interaction with The Source community. The kid's were still fast asleep as he checked on them in the spare bedroom.

Sanchez opened the front door and stretched for a minute on the porch. He took in a deep breath and enjoyed the quiet of the early morning. Sanchez headed left out of the rental house and followed a gravel path across from the compound. He ran about a mile up the road and came back the same way near the front of the entrance to the compound. Katie and Charlie had given an approximation of where they found Lindsey.

Sanchez ran through the wrought-iron gate, past the cabins, and to the right side of the meeting space. The sun was an hour from rising. The Source compound was mostly asleep, and not much activity around the grounds.

He checked his watch and didn't want to take too long with the kids asleep at the house. And didn't want to be seen by The Source community most of all. Blowing his cover would not help his cause. Sanchez found the shed in the back of the meeting space. He examined a path from the meeting space to the shed. He tried to create a scenario of how the suspect would've moved Lindsey from the meeting space to the shed.

A bird yelped and startled Sanchez. He rechecked his watch. He noticed a back door on the meeting space. And a second door on the back of the shed. He'd wondered if the suspect dragged Lindsey into the shed from the back of the meeting space. This strategy would block any witnesses from seeing the act.

Sanchez entered the shed and saw the uncovered Ford Falcon. He peeked inside, remembering Charlie said this is where he found Lindsey. He thought the car was surprisingly in good shape for sitting in a shed. A classic you don't see often on the roads any longer. Especially in the Midwest.

Sanchez flashed a light from his phone into the car. A part of him deep inside felt for the girl he'd never met. Thought about her loved ones back home. The worst part of the job, not making it personal and stuffing the feelings down. But he stuffed. Sanchez flashed to the kids' images on the wall in the rental and wondered what in the world these sick people were doing with these teens. Were they new recruits like Katie suggested in the coffee shop? Whatever it was, nothing good, and Sanchez determined to end it soon.

He searched high and low for a potential murder weapon in the shed. It was like finding a needle in a haystack without seeing the body or having an autopsy report. He wasn't sure the cause of death. One thing Charlie said was he didn't remember seeing a bullet wound. Not that he was looking for one. It also reminded Sanchez that Charlie was no detective.

Sanchez scanned the opposite side of the car. A shovel leaned against the wall. Above the shovel was a metal hook which appeared to be its landing spot. He placed the shovel on the hook, and it fit like a glove. Sanchez took a double take and examined a fair amount of blood on the blade of the shovel.

He pulled it down and got a better look. Definitely blood, and the question was if it was Lindsey's blood?

Sanchez heard a thump on the side of the shed. He yanked a small firearm from the waistband of his sweats. He raised the gun toward the entrance of the shed. A man nuzzled the door ajar.

Sanchez held the weapon trained on the intruder. "Who's there? Please raise your hands and show yourself. I have a gun."

A younger man wearing overalls peeked inside the shed and then came into full view. It surprised him to see Sanchez holding the gun. "Oh, man. Please don't shoot me. I'm just looking for some lawn supplies. It's mowing day. Who are you?" the man asked, unfazed by the armed agent.

Sanchez stuttered out a response. Not prepared to engage with an intruder. "I was out on a run. Came across this campground and enjoyed the scenery," Sanchez said, realizing his story was lame.

"Why are you in the shed? Are you lost?"

"I saw an open door and wandered inside. I used to have a Ford Falcon when I was in high school. I had to take a look. You know, nostalgia," Sanchez said, his hand shaking, trying to hold the pistol steady.

The young man in overalls said, "Okay... Can you put the gun down? It's making me nervous. I just need to check the gas and oil levels on the tractor. Is that okay?"

Sanchez smiled. "Isn't it a little early to be checking these tractors? Won't you wake up the rest of the camp?"

"I enjoy getting an early start. I won't mow for a few hours. Just trying to get ready for the day. Early bird catches the worm, right?"

"Yeah, something like that. Say, tell me what goes on at this place? What is this camp about?"

"We're not a camp any longer. I think the property was a Christian camp years ago. We live here full time now."

"Who is we?"

"The Source. We're just a Happy family living here in Boonville."

"Sounds interesting. I think family is everything. I have a wife and two kids at home. You have a family?"

"Oh, sure. I have five kids of my own."

"Man, you must have a couple wives to keep up with all those kids."

The man wasn't laughing. "Yep, I do. I know it sounds weird. But our community has a different way of doing family. We think it's God way."

Sanchez did everything in his power to not put a bullet hole in his forehead. He'd known of the polygamy and questionable practices at The Source which kept him all these months. He wanted these monsters to go away and not hurt any more people.

"No judgment. That's between you and God and your multiple wives," Sanchez said, placing the gun back in his waistband.

"If you don't mind me asking, mister. Why the gun? Boonville is a safe town. You don't need a gun for going on a run, do you?"

Sanchez glanced down at the pistol sticking up through his waistband. "Old habit. Go for a run, grab your pistol. I grew up in the city, and it wasn't always the safest neighborhood."

"That's an interesting story. Or you could be a special agent trying to destroy our community? How does that sit with you?" the man said. His jovial demeanor shifted to a stern look on his face.

The man in overalls grabbed the shovel against the wall and charged Sanchez. Before the agent could grip his gun, the blade of the shovel caught him across the right temple. Blood exploded from the gash. His head splayed open like a fish ready to be gutted. Sanchez laid in the grass on the floor of the shed.

The man in overalls spun the shovel in his hand and watched Sanchez bleed. Like he'd done this many times. "You're a liar, Sanchez. We know why you're here."

Sanchez tried to speak. His brain fogged, and the pain of the blow of the shovel was causing his head to throb with unbearable weight. The words in his brain wouldn't come out of his mouth. His mouth felt like they were full of marbles.

Sanchez said, "Go to hell. You'll have your day."

He blacked out.

The man in overalls checked the oil and gas in the tractors. They were at their proper levels.

He then dragged Sanchez out of the shed as the sun came up. He opened the back door of the meeting space. The same door where Lindsey Sparks would have her last thought on earth.

Chapter Twenty-One

The basement of the meeting space was damp and still. Sanchez sat on a wooden chair and shot open his eyes. The blow from the shovel caused blood to drip down the right side of his cheek. He scanned the dark room: cold cement floors and the smell of mildew.

Sanchez had no vivid memories of the last couple of hours, but he remembered the shovel and shot to the face.

A man came out of the shadows of the basement. He pulled a string on a single light bulb hanging in the middle of the room. Sanchez struggled to hold his head up with the pressure in his head. Duct tape tore into his hands and pulled on the hairs of his arms.

Sanchez squinted as his eyes adjusted to the light. The man came in close to Sanchez. He brushed the shoulder of the agent with the back of his hand gently. Sanchez found it creepy.

"It didn't have to be this way, Sanchez. We understand why you're here, and we don't like it. We found you on our property, which makes this much more difficult. When people leave us be, we leave them be. Not this time."

Sanchez hung his head and listened to the man ramble. He worked hard to lift his head and said, "Technically, this is public property. You don't own the campground. The city does. I've done my homework."

"Ah yes, that bull crap. We've been fighting that litigation for years. Everyone knows we bought the property from Life Change Camps years ago, fair and square. I will not allow bureaucratic nonsense from our broken government to force our people on the streets. You'd like nothing more than for our community to go away with the likes of the Dodo? Isn't that right, Agent Sanchez?"

"Couldn't have said it better myself," he said, as blood pooled up around the inch-long gash on his temple. "We know more about you than you know about yourself. The history of The Source goes back much further before your tenure. A time before it became corrupt."

"Look at you. A church historian. Not a good one, but you're trying."

"I'd hardly call The Source a church. A fringe cult or sect at best. Worst, a crazy community that controls the mind of young people to do your bidding. How is that for church history?"

"When I took over, I felt the community needed a fresh vision and a new direction. The old ways were too churchy and safe for me. I believe we're fighting for something much nobler. Something that will impact generations to come."

"We'll see about that. You have litigation and lawsuits aplenty coming down on you. Not to mention prison time and who knows what else."

Zebediah Mulvaney smirked. "Empty threats. We've been hearing the same rhetoric for years. When is that coming? Oh, wait, never. Our little community is much more powerful than you'd think. Don't think because we're country, that we don't have resources. You'd be amazed."

"Oh, I know. But that will be done soon. The cost to run your operation is staggering. Is that why you're desperate for recruits? Why you poach youth group kids coming into town? Is that your play?"

"Oh, Sanchez, you small man. I wish our relationship could've started on a better foot. But when I heard you worked for Jim Tanner, that simply was not possible."

"Why? Because he caught you in the act? He exposed the darkness that lurks in your community. When people feel threatened, they go on the attack."

Zebediah smiled and walked over to Sanchez. He bent down. His boots settling into a puddle of water. He spoke calmly. "We aren't hurting anyone. Yes, maybe our ways appear strange to a watching world. But the unenlightened aren't expected to receive the Truth. Your one of the unenlightened and have crossed a line. And we don't like when people come into our community unannounced and make judgments on us. Our community will determine your future."

Sanchez sensed the tone of Zebediah wasn't a bluff. "I'd be careful. Who says I don't have agents swarming this place right now?"

"Even so, we'll be ready. We are small, but we are mighty."

Zebediah yanked on the chain to the light bulb. The basement went dark. "We'll chat again, Mr. Sanchez. Enjoy your evening."

Chapter Twenty-Two

Charlie woke up first. He worked to get his sleepy eyes open as they were sealed shut with eye boogers. He could've slept for another three hours. After rustling on the air mattress and standing on the creaky wooden floor, Katie moaned. "What the hell, kid? Why are you up so early? I have a day off from the hotel. I planned to sleep until noon."

Charlie glanced at his watch. "It's not that early. Nine o'clock."

"Where's Sanchez?" Katie said, giving a yawn.

Charlie shrugged and peeked into the hallway. The bedroom door of Sanchezs' room was propped open with no signs of life. Charlie wandered into the living room, and a pot of coffee was simmering in the maker. Charlie shouted to Katie. "He's not here. Want coffee?"

Katie slumbered into the living room and plopped on the couch. "Get me some coffee, servant."

Charlie looked at Katie with wide eyes. "Excuse me? Address me as 'man-servant.'"

"Okay, man-servant. Extra cream and sugar. I'm feeling like a zombie."

Charlie opened the curtains to the living room to allow for some sun. The warmth of the late morning was heating the living room. He made a coffee for Katie and himself.

He sipped the hot beverage at the coffee table. "How does this work? Are we supposed to stay here, or can we leave?"

Katie shrugged. "I'm free to roam. I think Sanchez is more worried about you. You're the one that screwed up talking to that kid."

"You know the serious counseling I'm going to be in after Boonville? Remember when I left in the Honda, and Boonville spit me back? Bumping into Ryan is the least of our worries. I might need my dad's counseling services if he ever shows up. I wonder where Sanchez is? Yesterday was brutal, hanging out here all day. A man can only play so many rounds of Words with Friends."

"You play Words with Friends? What are you ninety?"

"It helps with my writing."

"Writing, what writing?"

"It's nothing. I do a little writing on the side."

"Like a diary? Charlie... please tell me you carry around a dairy. You'll never hear the end of it."

Charlie blew on his coffee to cool it down. He sipped. "No, I don't have a diary. But if you're referring to my journal, I have one of those."

"Journals are just guy diaries. Whatever, show it to me. I want to hear your deepest and darkest secrets. Is the diary pink?"

"The journal is brown, thank you. And I play Words with Friends for my short stories. It broadens my vocabulary. I want to be a writer if the universe will let me."

"Let's see some of these stories, Tanner. I've always wanted to date a writer."

Charlie sunk into the leather couch, enjoying the warm coffee coursing through his body. Waking him up from a terrible night's sleep. "So, we're dating now?"

"I said I wanted to date a writer. Show me the stories for validation. I'll determine our status at the proper time," Katie said with a smile.

"It's bad luck to show your stories to others before they're done. Besides, most of them are just ideas and concepts I'm working out."

"Chicken. I've never written a thing in my life. Whatever you have is better than anything I can do. Get your pink diary. Let's do this, Tanner."

"Journal," Charlie said. "I'll show you a couple stories. But don't laugh. I'm sensitive."

"Aren't all artists?"

Charlie set his coffee down and went to the bedroom. He came back to the living room holding a brown Moleskine journal. He handed it to Katie. "I have a few works in progress near the middle."

Katie opened the middle of the journal and read a couple entries. Her puffy lips moved along with a paragraph here and there. She then flipped to another page and read more. Charlie thought her lips were perfect. Not too big, and not too thin. Katie wore little makeup, and Charlie enjoyed her natural beauty. Most of the girls at school were always trying too hard to be pretty with makeup and scantily glad clothing. Charlie liked the girls who didn't care. Katie dressed comfortably and was comfortable in her own skin.

"Tanner... these aren't bad. I liked the one about the girl and her dad. That one has potential. You nail the emotion through the dialogue."

"Thanks. I'm still trying to find my voice and style. I like real people and actual situations. Not science fiction or fantasy. Nothing against Lord of the Rings. Can I have the journal back now? I've never shown anyone these stories, and I'm feeling uncomfortable."

Katie tossed the journal back to Charlie. "Don't feel uncomfortable around me. But I have one problem with these stories."

"What's that? You're a literature critic now?"

"My problem is they aren't done. How can someone enjoy them if you never share them? Seth Godin calls it shipping your work. You need to ship, kid. And I only date writers that finish their work."

"I'm still learning. One day the world will see my masterpieces. One day the world will celebrate the writer Charlie Tanner. Until then, I guess you'll have to wait to be my girlfriend."

"Fine. But don't wait too long. I have a line of cult boys waiting to take my hand in marriage, remember?"

Charlie blushed, playing with the journal in his hand. He then jogged to the bedroom in the back of the house. He found his duffel bag and placed the journal inside, thinking about the marriage comment. It made him happy.

Charlie zipped the bag and pushed it near his bed. As he pushed the bag across the floor, he noticed a small trap door in the floor. It was about the size of a doggie door at the back of a house. He pulled up on a bronze handle at the corner of the door, and it opened. He removed the wooden board and set it aside.

Charlie called Katie to come into the room.

"I'm not reading any more of your stories. Finish one already," she said, arriving in the room. "What is that? You find a Harry Potter portkey?"

Charlie knelt over the hole and peeked inside. He reached inside and pulled up a filing box. An aged yellow metal box came out of the hole. Inside was about twenty-five files. He dusted off the top.

"What are these?" Charlie asked.

Katie shrugged.

Charlie shuffled through the filing box and read through the contents. Each file had a name on the tab and photos and brief descriptions of each person.

Larry Nelson from Peculiar, Missouri.

Betty Marshall from West Covina, California.

"What do you make of this? Recognize any of these names?" Charlie said.

"Asking the wrong girl. Seems weird, though. That's not a normal-looking photo album. More like something the police would use. Looks official. You think Sanchez knows?"

"Maybe. But this box is old and hasn't been touched in years. It has an inch of dust on it. I'm thinking Sanchez has no idea."

"Good point. Probably just some old files from a previous owner. People hide all kinds of weird stuff in their homes. I remember watching Antiques Road Show, and someone found a painting worth a million bucks. Maybe we can get rich off the box?"

"You watch too much TV. What's with this house? Right across the street from The Source compound. Doesn't everyone know everyone in the Happy Town of Boonville? Any intel on this place?"

"Intel? You sound like Sanchez. And no, we don't know everyone. Okay, mostly everyone."

"Sorry, he's rubbing off on me," Charlie said, still examining the box.

Katie grabbed her chin and was in deep thought. She snapped out of it. "You know what? I have a vague memory of this house when we first moved here. Our community used it for, like, a guest house for visitors. I don't know much else."

Charlie read through another six files. "It doesn't say all that much about these people. I wonder if they are Source folks?"

He grabbed one more folder. The name said James Tanner on the tab. He opened the file. Charlie laughed that it was his dad's full name. He read a little more.

A photo of Charlie's dad about the age of eighteen was stapled to the corner of the file.

Charlie's stomach dropped. "Things just got more interesting. Not that we needed any help. That's my dad," Charlie said, tapping on the photo, and glanced at Katie.

Katie snatched the folder out of this hand. "Oh, snap. Your dad? Are you sure?"

Charlie nodded.

Katie found the lid of the filing box and wiped off the top of the dirty container. She read the smudged words written with black ink. "New Recruits."

"Here's your answer, Tanner. This box is new recruits for The Source. Your dad used to be part of our community. I'm guessing my assumption is right. This house belonged to The Source at one point."

Charlie rose from the ground. He grabbed his forehead and sighed. "The work my dad is doing is personal. He's one of them. No offense. What does this mean? He never mentioned being in a cult."

"We all have skeletons in the closet. Your dad's is in the floor."

Katie took one more look at the folders. One file folder popped up from the rest. She took a glance at the name. *John Brown.*

"I think your dad's work just got even more personal."

Charlie stared at the name and could hear the evil laugh of Sheriff John Brown. *Things definitely are getting interesting by the minute.*

Chapter Twenty-Three

Charlie paced the living room of the rental house. He mumbled things under this breath, poured another cup of coffee, and started downing a bag of chips.

"You okay, kid?" Katie asked, coming out of their bedroom.

"I eat when I'm nervous. How in the heck is Dad part of The Source? And where is Sanchez?" Charlie said, checking his watch. "He's been gone for hours. Isn't he supposed to be protecting me?"

Katie was amused by the recent information. "Let's be clear. Your dad *was* part of The Source. That was a long time ago. Young people come and test the waters of our community all the time. Who's saying your pops made it through the initiation phase?"

"What's that like? You guys drink goat's blood or something?"

"Yes, and then we drink eagle tears. Initiation involves some classes and a couple of ceremonies, for another time. I'm interested in how your dad knows Sherif Brown. Imagine what that was like? A young Sheriff Brown on the prowl. Terrifying thought."

"I'm going to be sick. Where's Sanchez?" Charlie said, staring into the bottom of a chip bag.

"Slowing down on the Salt and Vinegar chips will help. Sanchez is a big boy and works an actual job. He's probably doing special agent stuff. Whatever that means. He's going to flip when we tell him about the folders."

"If my dad was a recruit in The Source and something went wrong. I understand his obsession with this job. But I need to find Sanchez and confirm what he knows about Dad. This is crazy stuff. My dad isn't always an open book. He doesn't talk much about his past."

"That's normal. Older generations aren't touchy-feely like us. We share our entire lives on Instagram. It would horrify our grandparents. I also don't know how easy it is to slip into conversation that you belonged to a cult. I know the feeling well."

Charlie ripped into another handful of chips and stuffed them into his mouth. Chip crumbs fell to the floor.

"Tanner, please. Watch what you're doing. I have an obsessive cleanliness thing. I can't have you eating like a contestant on Survivor after starving for three days. "

"My dad's in a cult. I think I have every reason to stress eat."

"*Was* in a cult."

Katie found a broom and dustpan in a closet. She swept up the chips. Katie then gently rescued the bag of chips from Charlie. "I'm taking these before you hurt yourself. Stress eating isn't the answer. The Source has been around for a hundred years. The version you see today isn't how it's always been. I'm not saying it's all bad now, but I've heard from the old-timers, it isn't the same 'as the good ole days.' Don't make any rash conclusions."

Charlie watched Katie place the chips in a cupboard. He wiped chips from his face. "Fine, I won't jump to conclusions. But the thought of my dad and Sheriff Brown sharing a pizza is beyond comprehension. I wonder what happened?"

"What do you mean?" Katie asked.

"Something went south. The way the sheriff talks about my dad. The obsession my dad has with taking down The Source. You don't think the two are related? I wish my dad would show up and clear some of this up."

Katie had a sudden rush of excitement. "You have a laptop here?"

"Yeah, in my bag. What you thinking?"

"Get the laptop. The Source has a website with historical archived stuff. They give members privileged access to find family members and other archival information from the past."

Charlie ran to the bedroom and back with the laptop.

"You have internet?" Katie said.

"Sanchez gave me access to the WI-FI yesterday. Good thing, longest day of my life. Found myself down the rabbit hole of the internet. Did you know Brian Wilson from the Beach Boys stayed in bed for like three years?"

Katie gave a sigh. "Don't trust everything on the internet." She pulled up The Source website and entered her password. The page populated and gave a search feature in the top right corner. She typed in James Tanner. A profile page populated with Charlie's dad's name, photo, and some other links.

"Looks like your pops was only in The Source for a couple years. Age eighteen to twenty. I wonder what happened? Not a long stay. But also not uncommon either. People come trying to find themselves after high school. Some stay, some don't. Most move on to normal stuff like joining the rat race, starting families, and feeding their 401K. Actually, the reason my family left Florida. We wanted something better."

Charlie couldn't help but see the connections between himself and his father. Two men about the same age trying to figure out their lives. He related.

"I recall my dad talking about not going to college right after high school. Something about working a few years before enrolling in a state school. Maybe that's when he was in The Source. I still must know what happened between him and the sheriff?"

Katie clicked around on the site a couple times and pulled up a page of photos. She noticed a picture of Jim with an arm around another man. Katie pointed to the screen. "Looks like your dad and the sheriff were friends. Or they're faking those smiles."

Charlie leaned closer to the screen. "Perhaps. Pull up the sheriffs' data."

Katie typed in John Brown. A couple profiles emerged on the screen. She found the right one. "Appears the sheriff is about ten years older than your dad. He's been with The Source for over thirty years. Active member. I wonder if he was a mentor to your pops?"

"What do mentors do?"

"In Source world mentors help acclimate new recruits. But it's strange the sheriff had a folder in the new recruit box. Mentors are typically seasoned members who've reached a certain status in the community. Maybe the folder is just misplaced."

Charlie refilled his cup of coffee. Regretting the assault on the Salt and Vinegar chips. Coffee and chips were a terrible combination. "Let's say the sheriff was mentoring my dad. You think something went wrong between them? My dad heard or saw something he didn't like?"

"Anything is possible. The Source recruitment and initiation process is no joke. It's intense. Only about twenty-five percent make it into the first level of the community."

"First level?"

'Yeah, it's dumb. The community has varying levels. The harder you work and the more classes you take, the higher level you can attain."

"What level are you?"

"It doesn't matter."

Charlie could tell something was wrong with Katie. She leaned back in the chair. She tapped her nails on the table. "I have to tell you something."

"Go for it. Tell me you're part unicorn, and I'd believe you at this point."

"I've hinted at the good and bad of The Source. The classes are in the bad category. They use them in disingenuous ways to manipulate people. The classes act as a marketing tool. Is your life in the dumps? Do you want to be successful? That kind of stuff. People outside our community take the classes, and then they suck you into their orbit. But the classes also work as leverage to keep people in the community by taking more classes. Guilt people into staying. And if they aren't rising to the next level, if their lives aren't better, it's their own lack of commitment holding them back."

Charlie listened intently.

"The classes also cost money. Lots of money."

"Shouldn't cults be free to join? Most religious communities are."

"Yes, and no. They offer these entry-level courses to recruit people. These are typically free. Then they pull a bait and switch. They sucker you into more classes, which cost money. The more you pay, the higher level you can attain."

"That sounds shady."

"It is. You asked what level I am. Let's say my folks have little money. This limits our ability to go next level. They've made serious sacrifices to take these courses. But because we can't afford much, we've stayed at lower levels for years."

Katie's eyes were swelling red. "There's a lot of good in our community. But they treat my family like a second-class citizen because we can't afford the next level courses. I hate it. My folks have given up everything to be part of The Source. And they get little in return. I'm not sure what keeps them from bailing?"

"Sounds like it's not that easy to bail," Charlie said.

Katie closed the laptop. "True. I'm working at the hotel to pay for more classes. The only way I could work a job was to go on hiatus. You're not allowed to work outside the community unless you reach a certain level. You see, the pickle I'm in?"

"What a mess. Why go back? This all seems like a dead end to nowhere."

"I do it for the family. I have nowhere else to go. It's hard to explain, we've been down this road."

"Well, we're going to figure something out. My dad has a reason to have a personal vendetta against The Source and perhaps the sheriff. We need to keep poking the box and see what's inside."

"Now that I've divulged more of the crazy. Be careful. Like I've said, these people don't play games. Getting to the next level is everything. You can interpret as you see fit."

Chapter Twenty-Four

Agent Sanchez drifted in and out of consciousness. The side of his face throbbing from the blow of the shovel. Sanchez tried to keep track of time in the basement made difficult because his eyes wouldn't stay open.

How long did I stay awake? How long did I sleep? How are the kids doing at the house?

The basement still and damp. Duct tape pinned his hands back around the back of a feeble wooden chair. The tape dug into the hairs in his arms. Sanchez enjoyed the amateur mistake of using duct tape to imprison a trained professional. How to escape a duct tape restraint part of his early training as a special agent. Sanchez never thought he'd actually use the skill.

Sanchez raised his hands behind his back until they reached resistance. He raised them again and twisted his wrists to test how much give he had to work with.

Go time.

Sanchez raised both hands, cinched together with the tape to their highest point behind the chair. When he felt resistance, he took a deep breath. He then violently ripped his cinched hands down at an angle. The tape bent and flexed. The tension of the duct tape eased up around his wrists.

Sanchez repeated the move.

Each violent movement caused his head to hurt and nausea in his stomach. He chalked it up to the giant gash in the side of his face, which was leaking blood in spurts.

Sanchez lifted his arms one more time and heard a rip in the tape. A magical sound. The last raise and slam tore the duct tape apart enough to free his hands. The sound of the wooden chair slamming on the cement and the ripped tape echoed through the sterile basement.

Sanchez wobbled from the chair and removed the leftover tape from his wrists. He caressed his hands where the tape had ripped off a bunch of his hair.

He tried to find his bearings; the darkness allowing only a foot of vision. Sanchez reached out his hands like a blind man walking across a busy intersection without a cane.

Sanchez reached out in front of his body and glided through the basement, taking on the appearance of Frankenstein. Step after step, hoping to not make noise, awakening whatever Source leaders might be in earshot.

He stubbed his toe on something hard, stopping him in his tracks and almost sending him to the cement floor. Sanchez reached out his hands for a flight of stairs heading upward. The staircase led up and finished at a door with a crack of light coming under the door—the only exit in the basement, from what he could tell.

Agent Sanchez felt naked with no firearm and only the clothes on his back and a pounding face. He limped onto the first step, and the wood bent under his running shoes. Wood decayed, wet, and rotting out. Sanchez used his hands to guide his way up the staircase. Each stair cracking with each footfall.

He made it to the top of the stairs and placed his ear on the door.

Silence.

Was it morning or night? He guessed it was a little after lunchtime based on the time of his run, capture, and hours spent in the basement. Give or take an hour. The pounding in his brain ramped up.

Sanchez said a prayer and reached for the door. Praying nobody was on the other side. The nob turned. His heart raced, wondering what greeted him on the other side. Sanchez wasn't in any shape for a fight, but would do what it took to escape. He knew if he didn't escape and find the kids, things could turn nasty in a hurry.

The door opened to the outdoors. Sanchez blocked the sun with his hand. His eyes were on fire. The door which led down into the basement was across from the shed. He recognized the shed where he was pummeled by the shovel. Sanchez checked his surroundings, and it appeared clear to run for the shed.

A trick he learned in training. *Ditch your phone if you think someone is going to kidnap you. You might need it later if you escape.*

Before the altercation, Sanchez tossed his cell phone into the corner of the shed. Had a sense he might need it later. *Never lose your phone.*

Sanchez opened the shed and found the phone. The tractors and mowers were missing. He could hear loud machines in the distance. Hoped the noise would allow for a smooth escape.

He hid behind the shed, away from the entrance. Sanchez slid up against the outside wall of the shed and didn't see anyone. A row of trees led down to the outskirts of the property. He bolted for the trees and stayed low, running hunched over. The running wasn't helping his head as he worked to stay focused and not blackout. *Please don't blackout.*

The mowers and tractors echoed in the distance.

Sanchez zig-zagged through the trees until he reached the main road. A quick jog across the street, and he'd be at the rental house. He'd hoped the kids weren't too worried.

A car drove down the two-lane road. Sanchez dropped his head and stepped behind a large oak tree. He looked the other way, hoping he wasn't recognized.

He let the car get down the street and ran across the road. His head pounding like a balloon about to pop.

Sanchez limped up the driveway of the rental house. The house swaying and blurring from side to side. He thought to himself: *hit the one in the middle.*

He knocked on the door.

Nothing.

He tapped a second time as the messaging between his brain and hand disconnected.

Charlie opened the door as Sanchez collapsed on the porch.

Chapter Twenty-Five

Katie found a washcloth and some ice in the kitchen. She wrapped the cloth around the ice and placed it on Sanchez's head. He slouched on the leather couch, coming back to life. Katie examined the gash on his face. "Did you get in a fight with a lion? Good God, man. You might need stitches."

Sanchez forced a smile. "I'd prefer a lion. You should see the other shovel."

Charlie stood across from the couch with hands on his hips. "A shovel did this?"

Sanchez winced. "It was a big one. I'm no wimp."

"I'm guessing this isn't from a gardening accident? Where you been? We've been worried sick," Charlie said.

"Glad to see you guys still have a sense of humor. These Source people are light on the comedy. All business."

"What happened? You want to explain the hole in your face?" Katie asked, adjusting the ice pack.

Sanchez forced Katie's hand further down his cheek. He enjoyed the relief of pain. "You should see the other guy.

Nothing but a fleabite," he said, placing the ice pack on the couch, "The plan was simple. Get up early, go for a run, and see if I could get a better read on Lindsey Sparks. I checked out the shed you guys told me about..."

Charlie gasped, "You visited The Source compound? Are you stupid?"

"No, I'm not, thank you. It's what agents do. I had a gun and a plan. The plan was to take another look at the shed. Find a murder weapon if possible. Maybe not the best of ideas in hindsight. I don't want to blow my cover."

Katie laughed. "You think The Source doesn't know you're here? I'd think again, Agent Sanchez, with all due respect."

"Do you hear something, Katie?" Sanchez asked.

"Not specifics. They watch everybody. Boonville isn't Los Angeles, and everybody knows everybody's business. The Source are a paranoid people. Worried about losing their perceived freedoms."

"Should I be worried?"

"I have the same questions. Not sure if they're a violent people or just act tough. Our teachings center on peace. But nobody is perfect."

"Well, my cover is blown. And I'd say it's no act. Some guy slammed a shovel in my face. And the head leader kidnapped me and tied me up in a basement."

"Zebediah?" Katie asked.

"That's the guy. I've read his file. Not a good dude."

Katie stood off near the kitchen. Charlie could tell she was upset.

"What's up?" Charlie asked.

"Every time I tell myself things aren't that bad. 'You're just blowing things out of proportion, Katie.' I'm reminded of just the opposite," Katie said, pinching the bridge of her nose.

"Like what? The Source believes a lot of weird stuff. My

dad wouldn't waste his time if they were upright citizens. This isn't a new revelation, right?"

Katie was leaning against the counter in the kitchen, obviously fighting back tears. "You hear these stories about certain people in the community having tempers. A story or two about altercations getting out of hand. But you don't want to believe them to be true. You hear about the manipulation and classes used to coerce people and say, 'I'm just overreacting, again.' Don't we all want to see the best in people? Then when we see the worst, it's easy to live in denial."

"Zebediah has a sketchy past. He's a former Green Beret and left the military with a dishonorable discharge. Spent many years forming militias around the country. Preaching the anthem of freedom at all costs. Dabbled in a bunch of fringe religious groups. Found his way into The Source. Not exactly clear how he became the head honcho. Whatever stories you've heard about him are most likely true. Don't beat yourself up," Sanchez said.

Katie slammed her fist on the counter. "I know, I know. But I keep telling myself the good outweighs the bad. Like a wife getting beat up by their husband. This time it will be different."

Charlie came to Katie and wrapped an arm around her. She was shaking and leaned into his side. "I'll be fine. This happens about once a week," Katie said, wiping her cheek.

Sanchez said, "We're dealing with serious stuff here in Boonville. The Source is not all it appears. Promoting the Happy Life and Boonville being the Promised Land is a facade. And has been for many years," Sanchez said, reaching for the ice pack and placing it on his cheek, "Which brings me to Charlie's father."

Charlie perked up and left the side of Katie. "Did you hear from him? Please say yes."

"Not yet, we will. I haven't been totally open with you.

Please understand this is all for your safety. There's a reason your dad hasn't called you back all this time."

"He's busy at church. Emergencies. Pastor life. He'll be here soon. I get it."

"I know Jim is a busy guy. Juggling a lot of balls in the air. With two jobs, family, and other responsibilities. But his silence isn't because of busyness. I jammed up his phone, blocking incoming calls from you. I did the same for your mom. Too big of a risk. I told Jim I'd give the okay when things calmed down. After the accident, I panicked. I gave fake updates and ensured him you were fine. Your mom and dad are fine, and they think you're fine."

Charlie wanted to punch Sanchez in the face. But realized he wasn't a fighter and had no clue how to do such a thing. Yet the rage boiled into every part of his body. "All this time, I thought dad was ignoring me. Or doing what he does all the time, choosing ministry over his family. I even thought he was dead at one point. You didn't think he'd get suspicious and call the police or something?"

"All part of the risk. I was banking on the updates to lessen any suspicion. Jim trusts me. Like I said, it's all for your safety. When I came down here a few months back, I didn't know what to expect. Then the accident happened, and the more I learned about The Source, I feared for his safety, your safety, and even my safety," Sanchez said, rubbing his wounded face. "I feared if he came down, it could put you in more danger. The kids. Himself. I had to figure more things out before giving the okay. Your dad is unrelenting in wanting to take down these people. But I couldn't have him or you in harm's ways at this point. I hope you understand?"

Charlie left the room and came back with the filing box. He placed it on the coffee table in front of Sanchez. "When you disappeared, Katie and I found something you might find interesting. I think all talks of safety are off the table. Look," Charlie said, nodding at the box.

Sanchez leaned forward and opened the top of the box. He pulled out a file and glanced at Charlie with a puzzled look.

"Keep scanning the files, and you'll find something of interest," Charlie said.

Sanchez thumbed through the files and found Jim. "Holy cow. Your dad was in The Source? That makes things interesting."

"Yeah, it explains why my dad goes without food and only talks about the cult in Boonville 24-7. He's a freaking former member and BFF with Sheriff John Brown."

"Where did you find this stuff?" Sanchez asked.

"A trap door in our bedroom," Katie said, reentering the living room.

"This is like hitting the lottery," Sanchez said, scanning the documents like a kid at Christmas.

"I'd say so. Katie thinks the rental house used to belong to The Source. They must've hidden the files in the floor," Charlie said.

Sanchez continued to thumb through the files. He smiled with every new file. "This could give us everything we need to make these guys go away. I'll have to tell Jim," Sanchez said, shaking his head, "I'll have to make fun of him for being a cult member, too," Sanchez said.

Katie said, "*Former* cult member. Let's be precise."

"I'm sure all this is hard for you, Katie," Sanchez said.

She nodded. "It's hard and normal. I'm not shocked by anything with The Source. But when they're family, you live in denial, right?"

"We all do it. Whether you're part of a cult or find out your best friend is stealing money from his company. Like you said, you want to see the best in people. But I'm certain by our brief interactions that you don't want anyone hurt. Justice for the victims. I know that's what Jim wants too." Sanchez rose from the couch and laid a gentle hand on Katie's shoulder. "We're all hoping for a good outcome."

Katie welled up and nodded.

Sanchez reached into his pants pocket and pulled out his phone.

He dialed.

He then whispered to Charlie and covered the receiver. "It's time for Jim's assistance," Sanchez said, waiting for the phone to connect, "Jim, it's Sanchez. We need you down here tonight. Does that work? I also have someone that would like to talk with you."

Sanchez handed the phone to Charlie. He was almost in tears. Hearing the voice of his dad was the best sound in the world. For the first time since he arrived in Boonville, Charlie thought everything would finally work out.

Agent Sanchez received the phone and explained the missed calls and put Jim at ease. In the coming hours, it would reunite Jim and Charlie.

Jim had some explaining to do, and so did Charlie.

Chapter Twenty-Six

Jim Tanner rested his arms on a cherry wood desk in his office. The office he called his man cave. A place where he studied, read, prayed, and welcomed every interruption of his children over the years.

Jim reflected on the call from Sanchez as the sunset through the white wooden blinds. The call he'd been waiting patiently for days. And yet, a call which suggested another reality. He'd have to visit Boonville one more time. A place that caused a roller coaster of emotions even at the sound of the word *Boonville*.

He nervously played with a cell phone on the desk, spinning it in circles. Staring at it like it was going to come alive any minute. Jim leaned back in his leather desk chair and sipped on a Bourbon. June wasn't a fan of his occasional nightcaps. Jim told himself it would take the edge off the impending drive to Boonville. The place with a complex past. A place justifying a drink or two.

Jim took another sip and heard the door open.

June Tanner stood in the doorway wearing sweatpants and

a tee shirt. Her hair pulled back in a ponytail. She smiled, wagging a finger at Jim. She came into the man cave and paused about the middle of the room. "What is that brown stuff I see?"

"Nothing, dear. Just Root Beer. A little something to take the edge off. You act like I'm an alcoholic."

"I didn't say that. But be careful. Your Irish family heritage provides an added proclivity toward booze. Remember that one Christmas when your dad hit the Egg Nog a little hard? He was singing show tunes at the piano without a shirt on. The last thing we need is Jim Tanner dancing on the church piano at the Christmas service."

Jim sipped on the brown liquid and smiled, thinking about his dad. A hard man, often an absent man, but did the best he could, being a product of the Depression. Jim entertained the idea of dancing on a piano. "Maybe it would shake things up at the church. You know our people could use a little awakening once in a while. I'm fine, just a little nervous about the trip to Boonville. Leaving in a couple hours."

June leaned across the desk and reached for the small glass of Bourbon. She held it in her hand. "I'm taking this. If you're leaving, you need a clear head. No way you're driving in your condition."

June left the room and emptied the glass in the kitchen sink. She poured a Diet Coke into a plastic cup with ice. She came back into the study. "You're switching to Diet Coke. Will wake you up and flush your system."

Jim knew she was right. But he still was nervous. He took a sip of the Coke. "Every time I go to Boonville, I get nervous. I've preached in front of thousands of people. Married and buried hundreds. And seen the best and worst of people. But my nerves get wonky when I even think about Boonville."

"Is it The Source?"

"It's always The Source. But you know my spotty history with the community. It's like a force hovers over the town, and it won't relent."

June came round the desk and forced herself into the lap of Jim. She wrapped her arms around him and swung her legs across his body. "The work you're doing in Boonville is important despite your past. It's important to the people you're helping. And it's important for putting the dark stuff of the past behind," June said, staring deep into the blue eyes of Jim. She gave him a peck on his lips.

"Mrs. Tanner, easy. Don't make me miss you even more. I appreciate the words of encouragement. Sometimes you feel you're wasting time on things that don't matter. I'll feel a lot better when all of this is over. I need to finish packing and get my game face on. You'll be okay alone for a few days?"

June fluttered her eyelashes. "I'm a big girl. Don't think Mrs. Tanner is helpless without her man. I'm more concerned about you and Charlie. Make sure he brushes his teeth. And please eat a vegetable or two. It won't kill you. I know when you make these man trips, you inhale toxic levels of fast food."

Jim smiled. "That's why we have you around. You always keep us in line. No promises."

June slapped Jim's wrist. She gave another kiss on his lips and crawled from the chair. "You get packed, and I'll whip up some snacks for the trip."

"No healthy stuff," Jim said.

June ignored the comment and left the room.

Jim finished packing in the bedroom. He shut off the light and pulled a roller suitcase into the front room. June had a cooler of snacks prepared and handed it to Jim. "Some fruits and other snacks. Also, some more Diet Coke's to keep you awake. You're not the best night driver."

Jim gave a last kiss to June and let it linger for a second. "Say a prayer for your man. I'll need it."

"Always," June said, backing away from the kiss on the porch.

Jim fired up the truck and waved from the driver's seat in the driveway. His stomach a mess of knots. Jim peeked into the cooler and noticed a pile of bananas and apples. He smiled. He then fished for a sleeve of Oreos, grabbed a Coke from the cooler, popped it open, took a sip, and then jammed it into his cup holder. He knew the drive down seventy like the back of his hand. No need for apps or maps.

Jim arrived in Boonville about nine o'clock in the evening. He cruised down Main Street and scanned each side of the street with a few stores open at this point in the evening. His stomach turning. A heaviness weighing on his shoulders as he entered into Boonville.

Jim passed through the main drag and made his way over a bridge running across the Missouri River. The night was clear, and the cicadas were in full force. A symphony played across the warm Missouri evening as he rolled down the window of the truck. The calming sounds mixed with the dread of knowing what Boonville is to Jim.

He hung a left into the entrance of the St. Mark's Cemetery. The graveyard creepy as not much light present except the occasional flashes of headlights in the distance. Jim parked the truck next to a curb near a row of gravestones.

Jim stepped out of the truck, scanned the dark graveyard, sighed, and walked to a gravestone about fifty yards from the truck. He passed about a dozen stones of various shapes and sizes. Jim heard the crunch of flowers under his boots. Someone had left a bouquet for a kid only a couple years old. Jim thought about a funeral he did with a two-year-old kid that died of cancer. A life lost way too young.

A simple gravestone about three feet high rested at the end of a row of other markers. Jim bent down and took another deep breath. He wiped the nameplate clean from the dirt build-up from Missouri seasons. It had been a while since he visited the gravesite.

The name said: Melissa Morris 1970-1988.

Jim kissed the stone. "I'm so sorry. It never was supposed to be this way. I'll never forget you."

Jim dusted off his jeans and walked back to the truck. He held back the tears as he scanned the quiet roads of Boonville. He arrived at Agent Sanchez's rental house. He knocked on the door. The front light blasted on.

Charlie came to the door. They embraced like they hadn't seen each other in years. Katie made a joke about awkward man hugs.

Charlie asked Jim about the tears, and he said it was because he missed his son. But really, the tears were because of Melissa. *Not the way it's supposed to be.*

Sanchez explained his reasoning for blocking the cell phones of Jim and June. Charlie was waiting for Jim to lose his mind.

Charlie was sympathetic as to however Jim responds. He was just glad to finally see his family.

Chapter Twenty-Seven

Jim Tanner was a tall and slender man, but still had some good muscle mass from his younger years. He had gray streaks in his hair, but most of his hair intact. A smile that could light up a room and a personality that drew others to him. Jim had some toughness underneath his sensitive preacher side. Probably the Italian and Irish mix. It came out when hearing about Sanchez blocking the calls from Charlie.

"Please tell me you're joking? You wouldn't allow my son to contact me? Why would you do such a thing?" Jim asked, raising his voice.

"Jim, it sounds crazy. But things were getting heated down here, and I didn't want you to panic. I understand how much The Source project means to you."

Jim stood broad-shouldered in the middle of the living room. Katie and Charlie on one side enjoying the brief altercation. Sanchez stood across from Jim, standing his ground. "It's a good thing my kid is safe. Or I don't know what I'd do? You get those pictures of the teens? They have a good time at camp?" Jim said.

The room was silent. Katie glanced at Charlie and raised an eyebrow.

Sanchez spoke in a calm tone. "Jim, take a seat. Those pictures weren't for a prank Charlie was playing on the teens at camp. I needed them."

"Why did you need them? What's going on?"

"I did everything you asked. I made sure Charlie got into Boonville with the kid's safe and sound," Sanchez said, looking over at Charlie and Katie, "But Charlie and the kids didn't arrive as planned. I went to find them and found the van totaled."

Jim rose to his feet and pointed at Charlie. "Dang it, Charlie. This was a bad idea. I forced you into this. The family business isn't your calling, and I get it. Too much, too soon. I should've let you join that music collective for the summer," Jim said, biting his thumbnail.

"Dad, it wasn't my fault. A deer jumped out, or something. It was a total accident. It happened right down the road from camp. I'm sorry."

Charlie found a chair and shook his head. "It's not Agent Sanchez's fault either. He came to the scene, and I was gone."

"Gone? Where did you go?" Jim asked.

"And the kids were gone," Katie said.

"What in the hell are you talking about? People don't just vanish in the air," Jim said.

"I know, right? I've tried to tell them there's a reasonable explanation," Katie said.

Sanchez fought off a smile and tried to stay in the moment and explain himself. "I found the vehicle, and no one was inside. I assumed they'd gone to get help and were safe. I didn't want my cover blown, so I left. Jim, I know this sounds awful.

But you understand what we're dealing with here. I was trying to think big picture. We have to be smart."

"So the kids are fine, right?" Jim said.

Everyone hung their heads. Jim glanced up from his chair and noticed the photos on the wall. He got up and examined each one. "I'm going to answer for you. No."

A look of panic washed over Jim. "Please tell me everything is okay," he said, glancing to Charlie, "What did you do? We entrusted these twelve kids into your care. Please tell me I don't have to call their parents and give them bad news?"

Jim walked the line of photos. "Why is Lindsey Sparks crossed out? Please tell me why, now," Jim said, slapping the wall, shaking the photos, and almost knocking down all of Sanchez's work.

"We don't know what happened? I found her in a shed," Charlie said, holding back a tear.

"Dad, this place is jacked up. Something demonic is happening here. A lot of unexplained things. Lindsey is only the beginning."

"Only the beginning? Are there more dead kids? Please say no."

"No. But a lot of unexplainable things *are* going down in Boonville. Katie has been a lot of help navigating the crazy," Sanchez said.

"Who's Katie?" Jim asked.

Charlie nodded at Katie standing near the kitchen. "She's part of The Source, kind of. She's on a break."

"Hiatus?" Jim said.

"Excellent work, Mr. Tanner. How do you know about that?"

"A long story." Jim sat back down. He hung his head. "Not the report I was hoping to hear. Anything else you want to tell me?"

Charlie grabbed the filing box. He opened the lid and tossed the files of Jim and the sheriff on the coffee table. "Found these. Thought you might find them interesting."

Jim looked at Sanchez. "You saw these?"

He nodded. "Could be helpful for the case," Sanchez said.

Jim examined the files like they were sacred texts of the Near East. "Wow, talk about getting in the time machine of the past. I was so young. Young and dumb. Where did you find these?"

"In the floor," Katie blurted out. "Do you remember this house from your time at The Source?"

Jim nodded. "Sure do. This used to be a multipurpose house. We had visitors come and stay here from out of town. I might've even stayed here. Sometimes used for small gatherings. A lot of good and bad memories here."

"So why didn't you ever tell me about The Source? Kind of a big deal, Dad," Charlie said.

"When you're eighteen, you do stupid things. I'm guessing you can relate? The Source was different in those days. Not what it is today. But if you're putting two and two together. Yes, I spent time part of The Source community."

"You were in a cult? Never thought to mention it? 'Hey, son, by the way, I was once part of a crazy cult. Please be careful of cults, they'll mess you up.'"

Jim chuckled. "It's not like that. We didn't see it as a cult. It was a place to belong. A place to find a *genuine* family. Katie can tell you. These communities have a powerful pull. They're good at what they do. Whether that is intentional or a by-product, hard to tell. You don't know you're in a cult until you're in one. I'd rather forget that part of my life."

Jim continued to scan the different files.

"What about John Brown? You hear of him?" Charlie asked.

"Ha, do I know him? Why do you think I'm down here? We were friends at The Source. I say that loosely. He mentored me for a bit," Jim said.

"I told you," Katie said.

"A bit, what happened?" Sanchez asked.

"A long story for another time. Let's say relationships are hard. And you don't always see eye to eye on things. A good relationship fights for truth and what is right. Something happened, not making that possible. I only spent a couple years at The Source and moved on. Met Charlie's mom shortly after, and the rest is history."

Jim closed up the files.

"Enough time walking down memory lane. But I will say... Sheriff John Brown is a dangerous man. Sanchez will attest. He's not what he appears to be. That's why I'm working so diligently in Boonville."

"Believe me, not new information," Charlie said.

"Have you met him? Did he speak with you?" Jim's tone became intense.

"He hasn't hurt me. But the moment I got to Boonville, he's been messing with my head. Believes nothing I've said since being down here. I'm pretty sure he killed Lindsey."

Jim nodded. "Wouldn't be the most shocking news. Brown has done a lot of things you don't know the half of. Mind games are his thing. He'll use his charm to trick you into doing anything. Happened to me, too. But I won't fall for his crap any longer."

Sanchez cooked up some food, and they spent the rest of the evening catching up and telling stories. They all wanted to forget about The Source for an evening.

Chapter Twenty-Eight

Zebediah Mulvaney stalked the leadership council with his eyes and methodical movements. He paced the meeting room at The Source compound, contemplating the right words for addressing the team. He paused in front of the room like a bolt of lightning entered his body.

"What goes through our minds when we learn we have captured the enemy? When the fight for freedom is progressing? And then what am I supposed to think when I hear the enemy escaped?"

"Disgusted. This is a setback for the cause," a voice yelled out.

Zebediah yanked out a gun and waved it in wild circles. Pretending to act like a wild animal. "Disgust, yes, what an appropriate word. When I think about what happened the other day, another word comes to mind, wild. I feel like a wild animal, out of control and ready to strike. Tell me why I shouldn't end every one of you right now? I came to this community because of the need for change. I saw potential and handpicked every one of you. And for all I've done for your spiritual lives, this is the thanks I get? All the hours I've sacrificed to mentor you into a world-class organization. For what? How in the hell does Agent Rick Sanchez escape? Does anyone want to explain themselves?"

A young man in his thirties raised a hand. He tapped his boots on the floor, his nerves working overtime. "I'm at fault. We held shifts watching Agent Sanchez. I had to take a leak and left the basement. When I came back, he was gone. No excuses."

Zebediah smiled and then jammed the gun in the waistband of his jeans. "I'm going to put my toy away before I use it," he said, and then stood above the man at the end of the table. "Did I hear you right? You had to pee?"

"Yes, sir."

"How long does it take to pee?"

He hesitated, thinking the question strange. "A couple minutes."

"I'll round up to three minutes. You had a lemonade for lunch. Ol' bladder was full."

The leadership council laughed.

The young man loosened up, thinking Zebediah was taking down his guard and going easy on him. "Well, I had a lot of coffee earlier that morning."

"Coffee does it to me, too. I have two cups first thing in the morning. But, boy oh boy, I'm peeing like a racehorse the rest of the morning."

The man nodded and smiled at Zebediah.

Zebediah left the man and walked around the table, still talking. "So let's say your morning coffee filled that ole bladder, and you took a three-minute pee. Let me ask another question. How long does it take to get up the stairs from the basement, pee, and then come back to your post?"

The man paused a beat. "I don't know, like an extra sixty

seconds. It's not a far walk to the bathroom. It's at the top of the stairs."

"Let me get this straight, Mr. Little Bladder. You leave to take a leak. All of four minutes, give or take. And in this short time, Agent Sanchez breaks out of his shackles. Walks up the only exit of the basement... in broad daylight, mind you. And leaves the compound undetected? That's your story?"

The man hung his head. "I got distracted."

"Oh, the truth comes out. You got distracted? How did you get distracted, Mr. Little Bladder?"

"Molly was in the kitchen near the bathroom. She had baked some cookies. I ate one, and we started talking. Next thing I knew, we left the house and were talking on the front porch. I lost track of time."

Zebediah gently released the gun from his waistband in his jeans. "Now that's a story. I'll admit it, the women here at The Source are special. Those cookies of Molly's are to die for. I've had one a time or two," he said, raising his arm straight up in the air, "Something about your story didn't add up. No way someone could escape from the basement in less than four minutes. Unless the person on duty failed. Is that fair, Mr. Little Bladder?"

"I'm sorry, Master. It was my fault Agent Sanchez escaped. After talking with Molly, I came back, and the basement was empty."

"So it wasn't four minutes, correct?"

"More like thirty," the man said.

"Thirty? Wow, that's a big number. Not a number I'd associate with someone on the leadership council."

Zebediah continued to twirl his gun and wave it around. "What should we do, team? I'm not sure Mr. Little Bladder is worthy of being on the council. Should we discuss a permanent removal? This kind of incompetency is grounds for dismissal."

A man spoke up. It was Sheriff John Brown. "You're a lot nicer than me. If a deputy did this on my watch, he'd be gone, no questions asked. Agent Sanchez is a thorn in our flesh. We're so close to pushing out the enemy and getting back to normal life. Now he's back on the loose, and apparently, our friend Jim Tanner is back in town, too."

The room gasped.

"Since you're not as nice as me. What do you suggest we do, sheriff?" Zebediah asked.

"I have some ideas. But a vote isn't necessary this time. These acts are an unpardonable sin. Our Master gave direct orders to our council, and they failed. Not only failed, but ignored a command from the highest-ranking leader in our community. That's grounds for instant removal from the council and the family. Am I correct in thinking this way?" the sheriff said, glancing at Zebediah.

The other leaders were silent.

"Zebediah, put away your gun. I'll take care of him," the sheriff said.

The sheriff walked up behind the man sitting at the table. His massive size swallowed him up compared to his frail frame. The sheriff grabbed the man under his armpits and ripped him from the chair. The man yelled. "Please don't, sheriff. What are you doing? Where are you taking me?"

"You're in my jurisdiction now. All sins deserve justice."

The sheriff drug the man by his hair out of the meeting room. Zebediah and the rest of the council said nothing and watched the scene unfold.

"Let us all learn a lesson. You follow orders, or there are consequences. The sheriff will do the right thing," Zebediah said in a calm tone.

The council nodded.

"I guess we should find our visitors and make sure they don't escape this time."

Chapter Twenty-Nine

Katie finished her shift at the hotel and raced the Honda to the rental house. It was early afternoon as she banged on the front door. Charlie came to the door. Katie bulled over Charlie like a linebacker making a tackle on the goal line.

Katie reached for her knees to catch her breath. "It's happening," Katie said, sucking wind.

"What's happening? Calm down, I can barely understand you."

"I heard from someone inside the community. The Source is doing a Shaming in an hour."

"A shaming? That sounds terrible."

"I've never personally seen one. From our sacred texts, it's a public spectacle to scare the community into submission. Only happens when a member breaks a serious law."

Jim emerged from his bedroom. He glided into the room and gave a half-smile like he'd heard it all before. "I've seen one."

Katie glanced at Jim. "They're real? I've only heard rumors. Like an urban legend to scare kid's from doing dumb stuff. Should we be concerned?"

"Concerned for the people involved. The one I saw, they beat a guy pretty bad," Jim said.

"Shouldn't we do something?" Charlie asked.

"It's tricky. The Source has every right to practice whatever they want inside their community. It's like trying to tell a family how to discipline their children. They can do whatever they want as long as it's not illegal. The illegal stuff is another story," Sanchez said.

"Isn't that a cop-out?" Charlie said.

"No, it's the law. We're walking on eggshells with these people. We can't intervene without a warrant or probable cause of a crime committed. They have plenty of legal resources behind them to defend at all costs. Ask your dad about the barriers we've run into for this case. And we don't want to shake up the hornet's nest. These people aren't stable. I have the scars to prove it. We have to be strategic and not ruin all the work we've done so far."

"I don't care anymore. We can't let them shame someone if it's as horrible as Jim says," Katie said.

"You're right. It does sound horrible. But we're not getting near them right now. Let them do what they have to do. I've already blown my cover, and we're working on borrowed time. We have to be careful and ensure every move has a strategic purpose," Sanchez said.

"Screw strategy. These people are my family. It's happening, and I'm going," Katie said.

Charlie tried to talk Katie off the ledge. "Aren't you supposed to stay away? With the hiatus and all?"

"Yeah, but I have to go. I need to go for myself. I need to go on principle. All the stuff I'm learning about The Source from your dad and Sanchez is a different picture than what I've experienced. I'll hide out and leave unseen," Katie said, moving toward the door.

"You sure? You want someone to go with you for protection?" Sanchez asked.

"No, flying solo. I'm a big girl. I have to do this for myself. It makes little sense, but most of my life doesn't make sense right now."

Katie said goodbye to the guys and hopped in the Honda. Her heart raced, and her mind swirled with conflicting thoughts about The Source. She loved these people like a family, but her time away had opened her eyes to a new version of The Source she wasn't particularly excited about.

Katie knew a side road where she could park the Honda. Also, a back entrance where she could sneak up to the center of the compound where the Shaming was to take place. Even the idea of whatever the public shaming entailed made Katie's skin crawl.

A group of about a hundred people walked toward the center of the compound called Town Square. Katie hung back near a cluster of trees. She waited until the crowds settled into their positions.

Town Square had a temporary stage built in the center of a gravel area. A wall of chicken cages and fenced off pens that housed livestock of pigs, goats, and llamas surrounded the stage about twenty yards back. A small cabin functioned as the local general store for groceries, supplies, and other odds and ends were on the cages' opposite side.

Between the chatty people and noisy animals, Katie felt safe hanging back in the trees watching the event. The community of about one hundred women, men, and children gathered around the stage. Some were standing, and some were sitting. Katie noticed the vibe of the event wasn't serious and more on the light and airy side. People hugging and chatting like they were attending Woodstock.

A PA system was perched at the back of the stage with two large speakers. A man plugged in a microphone cable and found Sheriff John Brown off to the side. He handed him a microphone.

The man that allowed Sanchez to escape was chained shirtless to a board sitting vertically on the stage. He only wore blue boxer briefs. His hands trembled above his skinny body that was attached by a ring at the top of the board.

The sheriff tapped the microphone. "Is this thing on?" he said, with a smile, "Source families, welcome to our gathering. It's with great sadness that we must gather here this afternoon. I've been tasked as the point person from the leadership council to handle an unfortunate situation. We have a person in our community that did unthinkable things. Heinous acts that require us to be here today."

The crowd moaned.

"This person was not just a member of our Happy community. But he was also part of our leadership council. After our ritual here this afternoon, he will no longer be serving in this capacity, effective immediately. Please do not associate with this man or his family any longer."

More groans.

"It has been a long time since we've had to take part in a Shaming. Our community prides itself on discipline and commitment and follows the laws of The Source. More times than not, we have compliant and obedient citizens in our community. But once in a while, we get an evil seed. And today, we must witness this evil seed being punished for their crimes of insubordination. May we all learn vital lessons here today. What it means to be loyal and obedient at all costs."

"Amen," someone shouted from the crowd.

The sheriff walked across the stage to a cabinet about the size of a medium bookcase. He opened the cabinet, and a variety of long Indiana Jones-style whips hung on metal hooks. He removed one whip with a cobra face etched in the handle. The sheriff tested the action of the whip. He gave it a couple practice whips. *Snap. Snap.*

The crowd cheered.

Katie fought back tears. Her heart racing with anticipation. She wanted to do something but knew she couldn't. Too risky.

Brown holstered the whip in his belt and jammed the microphone in the man's face. "Before we begin our ritual. Anything you'd like to say to your family?"

Tears welled up in the man's eyes. His head hanging down, almost naked and exposed. Humiliated. His wife and two kids looked on about fifteen feet to the side of the stage, also crying. "I'm sorry, family. I made a mistake. That's all, a big mistake. This is not fair."

The sheriff smiled and wasn't appreciative of his answer. "Mistakes are what kids do when they spill the milk. This is no mistake. These are sins you have committed. And sins must be punished."

Sheriff Brown handed the microphone to the sound guy. He then reached for the top of the board, where a chain connected into a ring. He pulled on the chain and yanked the man toward the center of the stage. The chain grew in length, coming out of the board like a hose wound up and being released.

The man hung his head. Wearing no shirt, blue boxer briefs, exposed and vulnerable.

Sheriff Brown wound up like taking batting practice. He

took an overhand hack with the whip, landing a blow to the center of the prisoner's back.

A red line of blood immediately oozed from the wound. More blood followed by swelling on his pale back.

Brown took another hack at the man's neck. The whip wrapping around his sweaty neck and caught the corner of his eye. He yelled out in agony as more blood exploded from his neck and right eye.

The sheriff continued the attack until his back, arms, legs, and face were a variety of criss-cross slashes from the whip. Each slap of the whip equaled more tears. Each slap, more cries for help.

The wife shielded the sight from their children. She scampered behind one of the animal cages with the kids.

Katie watched from a distance, bawling her eyes out. The cheers and shouts of the crowd mixed with the noisy animals were too much. She was closer to having an answer—an answer to her future at The Source.

She noticed her family in the crowd. What did they think of the Shaming? Katie would stay for them, but not much else. But even her own family would be up for negotiation after watching the public shaming event.

The sheriff removed his hat and wiped his brow with a rag. He then wiped the blood from the whip with the same rag. Brown smiled and then placed the whip back in the cabinet.

Another man came onto the stage and unhooked the chains from the man. The prisoner wasn't talking or moving. The assistant dragged him away as his wife and kids ran after him.

Sheriff Brown bowed before the crowd. He then dismissed the family.

The crowds dispersed, and people went on with their day like nothing happened.

Katie hobbled back down the trail to find her car. She

wanted to beat the crowds before being seen. She could barely walk with her eyes filled with tears and nose full of snot.

She opened the door and sat in the Honda before firing it up.

Katie yelled at the top of her lungs and punched the steering wheel.

Chapter Thirty

Jim surprised the crew with a field trip. They resisted and were more concerned about their hungry stomachs. He bribed them with food if they humored him. The sun was setting over Boonville, and the winds heavy as they piled into the truck.

They arrived at St. Mark's cemetery after a ten-minute drive. Jim drove under an iron archway with the title of the cemetery plastered in the middle. Charlie glanced out the back-seat window of the extended cab. "Is this a cemetery?"

Jim didn't answer and focused on the one lane of cement leading through the finely manicured graveyard. He parked the truck and asked them to get out. They marched across the dozens of rows of gravestones following Jim, who hadn't spoken a word.

Katie straggled behind about twenty yards. She had worked a shift at the hotel that afternoon and said she'd meet up with them. She was not in a chatty mood and was still shaken by the Shaming event.

Jim knelt down near the grave of Melissa Morris. Sanchez

and Charlie stood back, watching Jim with intrigue. Jim took a deep breath and sighed. A sigh of nerves and a sigh Charlie had seen many times. A sigh for when Jim wanted to nail a sermon and the weight of the congregation on his shoulders. He said, "When you leave high school, life gets confusing. You're supposed to have things figured out. But how can an eighteen-year-old be asked of such things? I read an article saying the brains of men aren't fully developed until they're twenty-five."

Charlie said, "What's going on? You're being weird. Why are we here?" glancing an eye at Sanchez, who gave a shrug.

Jim touched the line on the gravestone between the two dates: *1970-1988*. "My high school basketball coach brought our team to a cemetery once. Close to here. He said, 'You see that line? That line represents your life. Everything that will happen between those dates represents you. Life is short. The question is: What will you do with your line? I'll never forget that day. Changed my life."

Charlie scratched his head, still not sure about the reasoning behind the speech. "Dad, are you okay? Is this like a mid-life crisis speech? This feels very Remember the Titans-ish."

"When I was about Charlie's age, I searched. I wanted my line to count. My upbringing wasn't terrible. But I wasn't allowed to ask questions. They expected me to figure things out on my own with little direction. The playbook already planned out for me. Get good grades, go to college, and get a good job. During my search, a guy at school told me about some religious community called The Source. He said it was cool, and I should check it out. I did."

Katie walked up during the speech. She peeked around the crew and examined Jim kneeling by the grave. "Did they suggest you take a class?" Katie asked.

Jim smirked, looking up at Katie. "You have first-hand experience. It's how they get everybody. The class was something about finding your purpose. Sounded harmless. I was a lost kid looking for purpose after high school. Why not see what these people had to say? It took little convincing."

Jim wiped the gravestone with his hand. He tapped the white line between the dates. "I got swept up in the place's vibe. Lost all rational thinking and drank the Kool-Aid big time. Took all the Source classes available and was mentored by John Brown. Then things—," Jim said, now choking on tears, "Went downhill. It wasn't supposed to be like this. Melissa wasn't supposed to die."

Charlie knelt down next to Jim. He placed an arm around his broad shoulders and rubbed his back. "You know this person?"

Jim nodded. "My line is driven by what happened to Melissa. She was part of the community. My first love."

Charlie released his hand. "First love? What does that mean?"

"The Source had strict rules about dating. Melissa was living outside the community in another town. The only way I could see her was to convince her to be part of The Source family. She started taking classes. But when—"

"But what, Dad? What happened?" Charlie asked.

Jim glanced up from his tear-stained face. "Melissa saw through the crap. She questioned the leaders and their teachings. That doesn't sit well with these people. She knew John Brown was mentoring me and had a bad vibe about him. She wanted me to leave the community. Melissa called John out. He didn't like it. Thought she wasn't committed to the community and was a traitor."

Jim wiped his eyes. Dirt and tears mixed across his unshaven face. "He killed her."

"Are you serious?" Charlie said.

"As a heart attack. Brown threatened me and said if I ever told he'd kill me, too. I left the community not long after. My family then moved out of the area to Kansas City. I carried this around for twenty-five years. When I started the counseling center, my passion for justice for Melissa grew. I promised her I'd never stop until Brown faced the music. My line is for Melissa."

Katie turned away upset and walked away. Charlie was going to console her, but Sanchez intervened and chased her through the graveyard.

Charlie shook his head, feeling the weight of the story in his gut. He touched the gravestone. "At least we know my intuitions weren't totally wrong. Brown *is* a monster. I could tell from the first minute I met him. You think he's behind the missing teens?"

"Almost 100%. John was older than Melissa and me. We were the ideal demographic of The Source. Low hanging fruit. They find these young kids from small towns searching for purpose and a family. They pump them full of lies and suck you into their community. These gullible kids drink the Kool-Aid and become the next generation of Source disciples. I'm guessing he has plans to brainwash these teens into becoming part of the family."

"You think he killed Lindsey?"

"If not him, most likely someone in the community."

"Why would they do such a thing? These kids have only been here a few days. Brown wouldn't have gone to those drastic of measures already, right?"

Jim shrugged. "Nothing is beyond Brown. He has a short fuse, and if anyone pushes the wrong buttons, he snaps. I've seen it up close."

The winds kicked up, throwing leaves and dirt around the cemetery. "Did you see that?" Charlie asked his dad.

"What?"

"A clod of dirt shot up."

"Probably just the wind."

A clod of dirt shot up in the air a second time next to the gravestone. Charlie and Jim covered their heads. Bullets were spraying from the opposite end of the cemetery. Charlie yelled for Sanchez and Katie to get down.

Sanchez hid behind a six-foot gravestone, secured his firearm, and shot wildly into the dark and wind. The sun had set, and the cemetery was nearly quiet other than the shots echoing in the distance.

Jim laid in the fetal position shielded by Melissa's gravestone. Charlie laid on the ground next to him. More bullets whizzed through the air.

Then they stopped.

Jim poked his head up above the gravestone. Charlie scolded him to stay down. Jim reached for his hand and gave it a squeeze.

A voice came over a speaker.

"I heard we had visitors in our town. I love when new people come to check out the Happiest Town on Earth."

The voice echoed through the cemetery, bouncing off the cement and gravestones.

Jim recognized the voice. He hadn't been in the presence of John Brown in over twenty-five years. But the voice was familiar. A voice that haunted him in his dreams.

"I came to visit our old friend. You remember Melissa Morris?" Jim said.

Charlie tried to shush him to no avail.

"Did you come to pay your respects?" Jim said.

"Many people come through our town. Doesn't ring a bell," Brown said.

"Wow, all these years, you haven't changed a bit. Tell yourself something is true enough times... and you believe your own news. Even when all evidence points to the contrary. A lot like those who watch Fox News."

"You know what, I recall a Melissa. If my memory serves correctly, you're no innocent bystander. You drove Melissa away. You failed to teach her the righteous path of The Source. It could've been a better outcome for Melissa and *you*."

"Go to hell. You're a liar, and your native tongue is lying. If I stayed and drank the Kool-Aid, I'm sure I'd become a miserable human like yourself. How's that working out for you?"

Sanchez followed the voice of sheriff Brown. He crawled behind gravestones and mixed in a jog and run until he got near the voice. The police cruiser was parked alongside a curb with lights off.

He snuck behind a tree and cocked his firearm.

"You could've been my partner running this town. Too bad you had to choose the darkness instead of the light."

Sanchez fired a shot, and it ricocheted off the hood of the cruiser. The sheriff fired up the vehicle and blasted on the lights. Sanchez fired multiple shots into the vehicle.

Brown sped down a long driveway near the exit of the cemetery. A bullet hit him in the shoulder. The car swerved a bit and vanished into the night.

Jim, Charlie, and Katie all stood up and hugged.

Katie said, "What I saw at the Shaming, and what I heard from the sheriff, is the last straw. I'm done."

Jim nodded. "We're here for you."

Sanchez huffed and puffed and found the group. "I got a shot on him. I think he's hit. But now we've awakened the beast. Time to call some backup."

Chapter Thirty-One

The group reassembled at the rental house. Adrenaline pumping after the shootout. Sanchez bolted the doors and formed a blockade with furniture. He was confident Brown and a mob of Source people were coming for them.

Sanchez called in help from some contract special agents. More protection warranted in case a war broke out. They knew they couldn't stay in the rental for much longer. Had to find another makeshift headquarters somewhere else in Boonville. Sanchez and Jim had seen enough to give credence for reasonable cause and ask for a search warrant.

Charlie gave Katie a hug. "Are you okay? How was the Shaming? As terrible as you suspected?"

"And then some. They watched it happen like watching the Chiefs on Sunday. The only thing missing was popcorn. All the stuff your dad said about Brown is true. I'm done drinking the Kool-Aid and pretending The Source is a family. Families stand up for each other. They're nothing but evil. I still have to convince my folks. That'll be tricky."

"My dad always says truth rises to the surface. They'll see the light soon. We also need to find the teens and get them to safety. This is a gigantic mess."

Sanchez worked the phones in the back bedroom and told everyone to listen for any action outside. He briefed the other agents who'd arrive in short order.

Jim felt overwhelmed and somewhat guilty for putting everyone in this predicament. The vision of the counseling center always to help victims of cult abuse. Not start a civil war with them.

Jim called everyone into the living room. "I need to say something... I'm sorry. This isn't what I had in mind. We've been rescuing individuals from The Source for the last few months. I never intended to start World War III. Agent Sanchez was my eyes on the ground. We needed enough evidence to prove The Source was not a legitimate religious organization. Proof they were committing crimes of various kinds. The sheriff being part of the community and his actions tonight only helps our cause. But please accept my apologies as this has become more of a mess than expected."

Charlie nodded. "No sweat pops. Let's say it's making my decisions for the future much easier. I don't think ministry is in the cards. Much too dangerous," he said, punching his dad in the arm, "But... We do need to find the teens. Any thoughts?"

Sanchez said, "The Chapel. From our intel, it houses new recruits at an abandoned Roman Catholic Church down the road. The Source calls it The Chapel. It's a creepy place. We're betting on the teens being held up at the church. The Source compound is coming up empty."

"I've seen the place. Katie took me there when I got to Boonville. The place with the smoke coming up from the ground? Creepy is an understatement. Let's do it," Charlie said, slapping his hands together.

"No way. You don't go waltzing into The Chapel unannounced. We need a strategy. They don't take kindly to visitors. Nobody quite knows what goes on down there," Katie said.

"When I was around, they used The Chapel for recruit training. Is it not safe?" Jim said.

Katie shrugged. "That's the problem; nobody knows. It's a big secret. A lot has changed from your days at The Source."

"Didn't you go through the initiation phase?" Jim asked Katie.

"Yeah, like seven years ago. Zebediah came into leadership right after we came. We were already done with our initiation classes. He changed things up since then. Everything is hush, hush, now."

Jim nodded and chewed on his nails. "Well, if anything we've learned from these sickos is two things. One, they don't like to be questioned on their beliefs and practices. Two, they love to prey on young people," Jim said, glancing at Charlie and Katie.

"What is that look for?" Charlie asked.

"Just an idea. How about you and Katie work the inside?" Jim said.

"No way I'm going into that haunted house. They're probably sacrificing goats in there," Charlie said.

Katie slapped Charlie on the arm. "They have bizarre practices. But sacrificing goats isn't one of them. Besides, they already know me, and Charlie's face has been all over this town."

Jim grabbed his chin. "Good point. How about disguises? Pretend you're interested in the community. Take a class, maybe find the teens?"

"We did something like this already. It didn't end well," Charlie said.

"What happened?" Jim asked.

"Katie dropped me off for an outreach night. I blacked out, and that's when we found Lindsey dead the next day. The sheriff and Zebediah were there. I'm certain they had something to do with it. The sheriff accused me of using drugs in the park. Had this total story made up."

"That guy is so full of crap. You didn't do drugs, did you?" Jim said.

"Really, dad? I don't even know what drugs look like."

"Okay, just checking," Jim pointed at Charlie, "What is Lindsey's last name again?"

"Sparks," Charlie said.

"Why does Lindsey Sparks sound familiar?" Jim asked.

"The Sparks are part of our church. Lindsey is a senior at East Kansas City High. You feeling okay, pops?"

Jim popped up from his chair. "No, something else. The name is stuck in my brain for another reason," he said, heading to the back bedroom. He came back with the filing box, opened the lid, and flipped through the files.

Jim tossed a file on the table. "That's it. What does the name say?"

"Sparks... Jeff Sparks. Who is Jeff Sparks?" Charlie said.

"I don't know. But Lindsey is a Sparks. Why would Brown kill Lindsey? Or maybe a better question: why was Lindsey at the outreach meeting like you said? The Source moves quickly on new recruits. But if we're talking only a couple days from the crash and the meeting. Not even a psycho like John Brown would kill a young girl that quick for not showing loyalty. What am I missing?"

"He killed Melissa Morris. Nothing is out of bounds for the sheriff," Charlie added.

"True, but it was over a year of battles with Mellissa before he snapped," Jim said.

He lifted the file and examined it again. "Try this on for

size. Somehow this Jeff Sparks is related to Lindsey. An uncle, a cousin, who knows? What if things went sideways with Jeff, and he pushed back on Brown? All these years, he's waited for payback. He then takes it out on Lindsey because of their family? A death by association murder," Jim said.

"Sheesh, dad. Not a bad idea at all. Only for one problem. The joke's on you. If what you're saying is true, Brown has been playing you the entire time. He somehow had to know Lindsey was coming down to Boonville with our church group. Brown then would've caused the crash, stole the kids, and made me out to look like a crazy person. Everything has a rational explanation, right?" Charlie said, glancing at Katie.

"The joke would be on me. I hope this isn't true anymore. That means Brown has been watching me for years. Waiting for the right time to pay me back for Melissa. I'll have Sanchez run some intel on Jeff Sparks and see what he can find. In the meantime, we need to find the teens."

Sanchez came running in from the other room. "Good news, help is on the way. I ran the idea about Charlie and Katie going undercover at the chapel. Not a good idea. Too risky. We have another idea. But first, we need a new headquarters. This place is compromised. I've secured one up the road."

Sanchez had the crew pack up their minimal belongings and headed for Jim's truck.

Charlie thought about the cemetery and his line. Whatever his line was, it appeared to be in a faraway land. It relieved Charlie he didn't have to go undercover with Katie. The chapel was too creepy for his liking.

Chapter Thirty-Two

Sanchez found a new hideout on the outskirts of Boonville. A barely solvent motel, Crazy 8, would serve as headquarters for now. Katie said the roach-motel only survives because of the occasional tourist passing through town in the middle of the night and drug dealers. The smell of urine and aged cheese also didn't help the cause of the *Eight*.

Sanchez paid to inhabit the entire motel for a week. He'd hoped the case would be done before then. A lady with a missing tooth working the counter was ecstatic. Like she'd hit the lottery. The Eight hadn't been fully occupied since the 80s.

Sanchez convinced five more contract agents to join the fun in Boonville. Sanchez and Jim alone and with little help from local police wouldn't suffice. He feared retaliation from The Source, and they'd simply be out-manned.

Katie was upset about the accommodations. She offered the Boonville Hotel but got shot down because Sanchez thought the center of Boonville was too risky. Assuming Brown and his Source cronies were on the prowl.

One agent, a portly man with thinning black hair, devised a

sting operation to enter the Chapel. They'd pretend to be Missouri energy workers out to fix an electrical problem in the area. They'd gain access to the Chapel by checking on their electrical panel. If The Source people refused, they'd threaten to shut off the power. Win, win. They'd snoop around and see if they could get a bead on the teens.

Katie and Charlie liked the alternative plan as it didn't involve them going inside the Chapel. Charlie thought anything that minimized death was also a plus. Sanchez got the rest of the team up to speed on The Source. They had plenty of evidence and probable cause to take The Source down at the proper time. Priority one was getting the teens to safety.

Sanchez found a local van rental company to use for the scheme. Two agents would drive a plain white work van and go undercover as utility workers. The men were wiretapped and recorded for the entire deployment. Sanchez and his team set up a makeshift command center in the sketchy motel with monitors, computers, video, and sound equipment. The motel was only a few blocks from the Chapel in case things went south.

Late morning the next day, the two agents prepared to enter the chapel. Sanchez got wind that some event was supposed to happen at the chapel that morning. Katie told him they didn't use the chapel all the time. The event would hopefully make access easier for the agents. He also thought the day time investigation would appear more legitimate.

They chose Jose Martinez and Ray Jackson for the operation. Jose was a former Iraq vet working as a contract agent following two tours of duty in Afghanistan. Ray was a middle-aged, semiretired agent and worked jobs as needed. He says his extra cash was for golf money.

Jose parked the van across the street from the chapel. The Roman Catholic building shined in the morning sun. Birds perched on the roof and watched as the men approached. A third agent Bill Paxton stayed inside the van to listen and watch the operation and serve as backup if needed. He'd also be communicating with Sanchez and the rest of the team at the motel. Paxton was the youngest of the crew and had a background in audiovisual surveillance from his time in the military.

Jose and Ray put on their hardhats and climbed the steps of the church. They adjusted their fake Missouri Energy lanyards. The birds scattered in their coming. Ray pointed to the right side of the building as steam came up from the ground. "What's that?"

"Sanchez mentioned something about a fire under the ground. I don't know?" Jose said.

"What did you say? A fire underground?" Ray asked.

"Don't worry about it," Jose said.

"This place gives me the creeps. Let's make this quick and get out of here."

"If you're lucky," Jose said with a smile.

Jose knocked on the massive front door. He also rang a doorbell for good measure. He held up his fake clipboard and tried to look professional. Whatever that was supposed to look like?

He knocked again, no answer.

The men turned to the van, and Ray shrugged.

Before they could turn back, someone opened the door. "Can I help you? Are you here for the classes? They don't start for another hour. Come back then," the young man said, about to shut the door on the men. The brown-haired man looked about twenty.

Jose said, "Sorry to bother you, son. We're from the electric company. We've had some problems in the area. Summer storms messed up some lines. We'll have to come inside your building and check a couple things. It won't take long, and then we'll get out of your hair."

The young man looked the workers up and down. "You said the electrical company? Can I see some ID?"

The men flashed their fake badges. He nodded.

"I probably should talk to my boss."

Ray interrupted. "It will only take a few minutes."

The man paused a beat and gave another look over. "Okay, well, you must make it quick. We're in the middle of something."

Ray smiled. "No problem, sir. We'll be in and out in no time. Just have to make sure your system is up to code and working fine."

The young man opened the door wide and ushered them into the lobby. Beyond the lobby was another set of doors leading to the chapel with pews and a stage. The stage had drums, guitars, and microphones on stands. Nothing in the chapel looked weird. Jose thought the space looked like the Catholic church he grew up in.

"You have mass on Sundays?" Jose asked.

"Not exactly. We use our chapel for special gatherings throughout the week. Teach classes and such. You guys interested in taking a class? We help people find their purpose," the young man said, lighting up with a grin.

"We're good," Jose said.

Ray wondered what kind of gatherings but let it pass. He didn't want to get too chatty and blow their cover. They were here for one reason, and that was to find the teens.

"If you could show us your electrical panel, we'll get to work and get out of here," Ray said.

The young man said, "Down in the basement. Follow me."

The men veered to the right, passing the chapel and finding a set of stairs spiraling down into the bowels of the church. It smelled of mildew and dust. The young man seemed nervous and peered back at the men after every few steps. "Pardon our mess. We're doing some renovations."

Ray smiled and glanced back to Jose trailing behind. "No problem. If anyone knows messes, we do. Our job always brings us into interesting places. We've seen it all."

The men reached the bottom of the stairs and headed left down a hallway. An air conditioner unit fired up and sounded like it was crying out for help. They went further, passing a boiler and rows of shelves with various boxes, tools, and other supplies stacked to the ceiling.

They finally reached a door that opened into a utility room with two long panels of breakers and wires coming out of the top. Jose reached into his pocket. "Oh, man. I forgot a tool in the van. I'm going to head back. I think I can find my way."

The young man nodded and opened the panel to the electrical box. Jose rushed out of the room and back through the basement. Ray struck up a conversation with the young man to keep him from leaving the room. He asked about his family and the classes. And then asked if the electrical was upgraded. The kid had no idea.

Jose walked down the hallway and yanked a flashlight from his belt. He trained the light down a hallway that led to the right. The opposite direction of the utility room. He glanced back a couple times, making sure nobody was coming.

The gasping air conditioner made it hard to hear.

Ray continued to make small talk with the man in the utility room. The young man appeared frustrated and wanted to leave and let him work. Ray tried hard to keep him occupied, giving time for Jose to snoop around.

Jose walked to the end of the hallway and found a room with a door. A sign said: *New Recruits*. Jose wiggled the handle, and it cracked open.

He peeked inside and noticed a low humming sound. Not like the air conditioner, more like the buzz of fluorescent lights in an office. He found a light switch and turned it on.

Along the walls of the room were eleven chairs. And sitting in these eleven chairs were teenagers. Boys and girls. Each teen had a globe over their heads and wires coming out into electrical outlets in the wall. Jose assumed the humming was coming from the globes above the kids.

Jose stood near the door and didn't know what to do. The teens weren't speaking and had their eyes closed. *Were they dead? Sleeping? What in the heck is on their heads?*

Jose panicked and texted Sanchez. He told him he found the teens. Sanchez asked if they'd seen him. He said no, and they appeared to be sleeping. Sanchez said to get out of the building, and they'd work on a rescue plan. Sanchez was concerned about making a scene if the agents tried to rescue the teens. Too many unknowns in the building.

Jose took one more look at the teens, wondering what the machines were for. He shut off the light and closed the door.

"What are you doing?" the young man said.

Jose grabbed his chest as he almost had a heart attack seeing the kid near the door. "What an idiot I am. I got lost on my way back to the van. This church building is full of twists and turns."

"Yes, it gets confusing," the young man said, pulling out a set of keys and locking the door. "You're not supposed to be down here. I can get in trouble."

"Sorry, friend. I'll get out of your hair. The rest of our work will be outside, I promise."

Ray rolled up behind them. "I'm all good. Got everything I needed. We'll get out of here and let you get to your classes."

"Didn't you need a tool?" the young man asked.

"I think we're good. I got what I needed," Ray said.

"Thanks for your time. We'll finish up outside, and you have a nice day."

"You sure you don't want to try a class?" the young man said.

Jose did everything in his power not to slap the guy. "Nah, man. We'll find our purpose elsewhere."

The young man scratched his head. "Suit yourself."

Ray and Jose hustled up the stairs, down the church steps, and jumped into the van.

Jose said to the agent in the van, "You will not believe what I saw in the basement."

Chapter Thirty-Three

In the van, the audio-visual guy flipped a monitor toward Jose and Ray as they hopped into the van. "What was that in the basement? Were those kids getting a perm or getting their brains sucked out?"

Jose turned to the back seat and worked on his seatbelt. He told Ray to drive. "That takes brainwashing to an entirely different level. On the bright side, we found the teens. The cult counselor is going to have his hands full after this one."

The video surveillance guy, Bill, said, "My video was grainy. Were the kids hooked to those machines?"

Jose nodded.

"Machines? What kind of crazy people are these? I'm not sure about the laws. But hooking teenagers to brainwashing machines has to be a felony, right?" Ray said.

"No doubt. Get back to the motel and see what Sanchez wants to do. I can't work these jobs anymore after seeing stuff like that. I like the white-collar crimes. Less messy," Jose said, staring at the road.

The three men rode in silence until they rolled into the parking lot of the Crazy 8 Motel.

Sanchez was waiting out in front of room 227. He waved the men from the van over into the room. They grabbed various seats, and Jose sat on the bed. "I'm not sure what to do with what I just saw, boss," Jose said, hanging his head, "I need a beer."

"We're dealing with some whackos—a first for all of us. Tell me more," Sanchez said, taking notes.

"I don't know, man. I only caught a brief glimpse. Didn't want to blow our cover. Eleven kid's sitting around the room strapped to chairs. Had this electrical contraption over their heads. They hooked it up to power. I don't know what it was doing, but it didn't look good. The young kid who let us in the chapel found me snooping around. Just had shut the door when he found me. Don't think he suspected anything. I said I made a wrong turn."

Bill said, "I got video. It's grainy, but you can get the picture."

"Is that a video guy joke? Get the video up," Sanchez said.

Bill went out to the van and came back with a laptop. He opened it up, and the men sat on the bed around the machine. Bill pointed to the screen. "Jose enters the room. He hits the lights, and you can see the teens lined up around the room. Those machines are freaky, right? You know anything about these devices?"

Sanchez said, "My guess is something like the Scientologists use. They call them E-Meters. The Source's version are called S-Meters. From my research, they don't work. The science backing them is suspect at best."

"Do they brainwash the kids?" Bill asked.

"It's some kind of therapy that's supposed to erase bad memories or suffering from the past. I read some stuff on former

Scientologists that say it's a bunch of crap. Let's hope it's true for the teen's sake. I'll see what Jim knows. He's the expert."

The other men nodded.

Sanchez examined the computer screen. "I'm counting eleven teens. I've looked at the photos enough to say they're the teens from the church group. One step closer. We just need to safely remove them, call it Phase Two."

Sanchez took a hard swallow. "Were they alive?"

"I think so. Their eyes looked weird. But I'm guessing so," Jose said.

"Jim can shed more light on the situation. He's with a client right now next door."

"Client?" Ray asked.

"One of The Source people is next door. Jim's been helping this girl for a couple months."

"You think she could shed light on the brainwashing machine?" Jose said.

Sanchez texted Jim.

Chapter Thirty-Four

Jim slouched in a chair in Room 228, and a young girl about twenty-five sat across in an identical chair. Her brown hair sat on her shoulders. The bags under her eyes showing a rough few weeks or years.

She avoided eye contact with Jim. More interested in playing with her cuticles and staring out the front window of the dingy motel room.

"Tell me how you're doing today," Jim said in a polite tone.

She stared at the ground and tapped her fingers on her jeans. "I'm fine."

"Can you give me more? What does it feel like to be free from The Source? Does that bring joy in your life being free?"

"Depends on the day. It's hard admitting this part. I thought I'd feel better. It comes in waves."

"What part is hard?" Jim said, leaning forward.

"The Source is not a good place. But they were my family for a long time. I had to get out. But I didn't expect things to be this difficult. I thought when abusive marriages ended, you'd instantly feel better. I see why women run back to their abusive husbands. It's all they know," she said, biting her thumbnail.

Jim smiled at the young girl. "This is a common tale. Nothing you're saying is out of the ordinary. Family ties are a hard thing to break. But sometimes, when the family is toxic, the break is necessary. These feelings will subside with time and distance. You're only a few months out of the community. What else do you want to talk about today?"

"A low-level hum of guilt. How could I've been so gullible? Wish I never took those class years ago. I should've said no and went on with my life. I knew deep in my bones things were off. But I wanted to find a purpose, and they promised it was possible," she said, wiping a tear sliding down her cheek.

Jim nodded. "Don't feel guilty. These people are manipulation artists. I know the classes well. Making big promises and never delivering."

"How do you know about the classes?" she said.

"I've heard other clients from The Source talk about them. They sound like a bunch of nonsense."

"Yeah... it's like enough truth to make it sound plausible. But when you get into the deep weeds, it makes little sense. Nothing in your life changes, and they blame you for your lack of success."

Jim nodded.

The girl was loosening up and locked in with Jim a bit more. She looked around the dingy room with an orange carpet, yellow curtains, and outdated furniture. "Why are we doing our session here today, again?"

Jim leaned back in his chair and crossed his arms. "It's a long story. We lost our other meeting space. But I also need your help. We've been working hard to help people like yourself find freedom from the grip of communities like The Source. We're close to shutting down The Source forever."

The girl's eye widened as she nodded.

"I guess that's good, right? What can I do to help?"

Jim held up a finger. "Let me get a couple of my associates next door."

Jim left the room and grabbed Sanchez and the other agents that worked the chapel operation.

They entered the room and spread out. The young girl glanced up and shifted in her seat. The burly men made her feel intimated. "Who are these guys?"

"Just some friends helping me stop The Source from hurting more people like you. Can they ask you a few more questions?"

She nodded.

Sanchez reached out a hand. "What's your name?"

"Lisa Rollins," she said, returning the gesture.

"I'm Agent Sanchez, and this is Agent Jose, Ray, and Bill."

She gave a weak wave to the men.

"This won't take long. We're trying to get accurate information for our case. The better data we have, the better strategy we can take in stopping The Source from hurting more people. Is it true you were part of The Source?"

"Yes. For seven years," she said.

"Good, thanks," Sanchez said, trying to keep the situation calm. He scratched a note in a small notebook.

"Why did you leave?" Sanchez asked.

She glanced at the floor and back to Sanchez. Her lip quivered. "They hurt me."

"How so?" Sanchez asked.

"They promise abundant life, and yet they take away your life. Promise freedom, but only add more rules and laws. I lost all my friends and family. Cut off from the outside world," she said, wiping a tear.

"I'm sorry. How did they steal your freedoms? What does that mean to you?" Sanchez asked.

"Being cut off from the outside world is bad enough. But they steal your mind. They manipulate your brain. You question everything and can't even trust your own thoughts. You become a prisoner of your own mind. And don't get me started if you question a leader."

"Any leader in particular?"

"Zebediah Mulvaney. John Brown. To tell the truth, these are the worst ones. None of the other leaders on the council are like these guys."

The woman chewed on her thumbnail and wiped another tear. "Are we done now? This is getting hard. I don't enjoy bringing up the past. I'm trying to move on from this nightmare."

Jim said, "Almost done, sweetie. This is helping my associates bring justice to Boonville."

"How did Mulvaney and Brown hurt you?" Sanchez asked.

"Nothing physical. All mental. They make you distrust your own thoughts. You say something true, and they deny it. Skilled manipulators these ones."

Bill slid a laptop on a table near the woman. He tapped on the keys. "Would you help us with something?"

She nodded.

"What should we make of this?" Bill showed the video of the teens hooked to the machines.

The women turned away. She stood up from the chair and pointed to the computer. "Don't be fooled with the classes and the promises of an extended tight-knit family. That's what they do to mess with your brain. Every recruit gets hooked up to an S-Meter."

"S-Meter? Is that like the Scientologist E-Meter?" Jim said.

"I don't know about the E one. But this thing is pure evil.

The mentors monitor your brain waves and emotions with the meter. It's supposed to help you forget the past hurts in your life. Pretend they didn't happen so you can live a purposeful future. I think the machine brainwashes you and mixes the wires in your head."

Sanchez took notes, and Jim sat back, intrigued with the recent information.

"I think we have enough for the day. Thank you, Lisa, for your time. What you shared is not only good for your own healing, it will help us stop these monsters before they harm any more people."

Lisa stood up and addressed the room. "Be careful. These people will not lie down easily. And I'd rescue those kids soon before they end up like me. You still have time."

"Thanks for the advice, and we appreciate the time," Sanchez said.

The other agents thanked her and left back to Room 227.

Chapter Thirty-Five

Charlie tossed and turned all night. He thought about a conversation with his dad. They chatted about Lisa in broad strokes as to not break client-counselor privileges. He heard a lot of Katie's story in Lisa's. A desire to leave The Source and a strong pull to stay. Charlie understood from his experience with church that family ties are hard to let go of regardless of how healthy or terrible the family is.

He also tossed and turned because the voices were back. Charlie sat up in bed after going in and out of consciousness. In and out of reality and the nightmare. The voices real and loud and clear despite the foggy memories of the last week. Like people in the room whispering in his ear.

We're here to help you. Trust us. Don't listen to the demonic voices of the world. Everything you need is inside our family. You'll be safe. We will be your family.

Charlie slid out of bed. He then pulled the curtain back of the front window of the motel room. The parking lot mostly empty except for the cars and trucks of the agents and a front desk manager for the Crazy 8 Motel. A beat-up red Toyota Corolla.

He closed the curtain and headed for the shower, trying to wash off the pain of the last week to no avail. Charlie's body still sore but not with the same intensity after the crash. Ribs and an ankle lingering with tenderness. He cranked up the heat in the shower and let the water rush across his body. Charlie hung his head and prayed for healing.

The team led by Sanchez were planning a rescue of the teens later in the morning. After speaking with Lisa and Katie, it was obvious, the least amount of time the teens were on S-Meter's, the better. Nobody was confident as to the effectiveness of the machines, but it was too risky to find out.

Charlie wanted to stay in the shower for days. The heat and stillness a comfort for his soul. He thought about the plan. A plan involving himself. The looming stress of the day heightened because he was going to be the catalyst for the raid on the chapel. Sanchez's plan figured Charlie would be the least threatening for getting inside the facility. He'd wear a disguise and knock on the front door of the chapel. While Charlie distracted The Source member, the agents would rush inside, rescue the teens, and shut down The Source for good.

Sanchez knocked on the door of Charlie's room about 7 AM. Charlie finished putting on his jeans and a Led Zeppelin tee shirt. He sported a Kansas City Chiefs hat and dark shades. Sanchez wasn't concerned about a meticulous disguise as he said: *the hit will be clean and fast.*

Charlie opened the door.

"You good, kid?" Sanchez asked, sipping a coffee, "Nice disguise. Is it Halloween? You look like a serial killer. They'll never suspect a thing," Sanchez said, entering the room.

"I feel ridiculous. I'm not a big hat guy," Charlie said,

adjusting his cap and staring into a mirror above a bank of drawers.

"You promise I'll be safe? Promise to get the teens out of there fast, clean, like you said?"

Sanchez gave a thumbs up. "I can't promise anything. But what I can promise is the smell in this room is rank. Did someone die in here?" Sanchez said, plugging his nose. "I also had your father sign a waiver."

"A waiver? For what?"

"Standard agent stuff. We don't want to get sued if you skin your knee or fall down. Or you know, get shot."

"Shot? Who's getting shot?"

"Nobody. I'm messing with you. We'll keep you safe and get the teens out with no problems. I promise, maybe," Sanchez said, crossing himself.

Sanchez could tell something was bothering Charlie. "Everything else good? Your face is telling a different story."

"I heard those voices again last night."

"Like the crash dream?"

"Yeah, except no crash, just the voices. They freaked me out. It's like someone's in my room speaking to me."

Sanchez slapped Charlie on the arm. "At this point, water under the bridge. We found the teens, and that's all that matters. Whatever happened after the crash is irrelevant and might be a mystery until we die. But justice will be served, and that should make us all happy. Right?"

Charlie nodded. "Sure, I guess so. But there's a ton of stuff in this town that makes little sense."

Sanchez messed with Charlie's hat and made it crooked. "Most of life is unexplainable, kid. Just stay calm, and do what we talked about, and everything will be fine. In and out, clean and fast. We'll be home before dinner."

"Promise?"

"No promises. But justice will be done, and that's worth fighting for. "

Chapter Thirty-Six

Sanchez loaded up the van with firearms. The other five agents piled into the van, chatting and giddy like it was their Super Bowl. And it was their Super Bowl for their line of work. Nothing better to see the bad guys go down. The men were all tired and ready for this all to be over.

The Crazy 8 Motel was only a few blocks from the chapel. Charlie was going to walk and pretend to be a lost traveler. He'd knock on the door and ask for directions. The plan didn't need to be complicated because they were going to be *clean and fast*.

Charlie walked along a gravel path near the road as the van passed and found a parking spot across from the chapel. He adjusted his hat, checked both ways, and crossed the street to the steps of the chapel. He climbed the steps to the church.

Charlie's heart was in his throat. He tried to calm his nerves with deep breaths. He adjusted his Chiefs hat a second time and then played with an earpiece used for communication. The agents set up Charlie with an iWatch connected to an earpiece for instructions as needed.

Everything looks clear. Stay calm and follow the plan. The earpiece chirped.

Charlie nodded and found no comfort from the comment. Calm and a heart beating out of his chest didn't seem to jive together.

Charlie stood in front of the wide double doors of the chapel. Birds gawked from the top of the roofline. He glanced up and gave a weak smile. Not helping the calm.

He took a deep breath and knocked and waited. Tapped his sneakers on the cement entryway. He fiddled with the watch and looked around the property.

Charlie knocked a second time.

He leaned in close to the door to see if he could hear any noises inside the building. Charlie was getting impatient, and his nerves were unstable with each passing second.

The lockset clicked, and the door slowly opened.

Charlie startled and jumped back from leaning against the door. He collected himself and tried to form some coherent words. Heart beating in his neck, causing his face to redden.

"Hello, my name is Ricky Rayburn. I'm not from the area. Was wondering if you could help me with some directions? I appear to have taken a wrong turn somewhere."

A young man about twenty gave Charlie a stare down. He looked beyond Charlie and glanced at the van across the street. "You on foot?"

"Yes, sir. I love walking in the early mornings before things heat up. Best way to see the world is on foot. Thought a friendly church like yours could help a brother out. I'm religious too," Charlie said, realizing he was rambling.

The young man was amused with the banter of Charlie. He pushed the door open a little more and crossed his arms, leaning against the heavy door. "Where you headed to?"

"I'm looking for Main Street."

Main Street was the code word for the agents to exit the vehicle and rush the front doors. Charlie was supposed to use the word when he felt things were safe.

"Main Street, huh? Unfortunately, that's in the center of town. A good thirty-minute walk from here."

Charlie emphasized Main Street again, "Are you sure *Main Street* isn't closer? I swear it was near the river. Isn't the river closer than thirty minutes away?" Charlie said, turning toward the van across the street and turning quickly back. The agents weren't leaving the van. Charlie's heart was pumping. "Main Street, oh Main Street, how I'd love to get to Main Street," Charlie said, with a crazy look in his eye.

The young man held up his hands. "I told you it's a thirty-minute walk. Just follow sixty-seven highway around, and you'll hit it. Are you okay, man? You're acting strange. I can give you a ride if you'd like."

Charlie turned toward the van. No agents. *What is wrong?* He turned back to the door.

"No, I'm good. Just want to get to Main Street."

The young man repeated himself and offered a ride. Charlie noticed him reaching near his belt loop in his jeans. His face shifted from smiling to an intense focus. Like he was trying to solve a math problem.

The young man raised a hand above his head. A small object. A long and skinny object.

Charlie glanced up to the syringe glistening in the Boonville sun. He tried to press a button on the watch and yell for help. The agents were silent. *Where are they?*

The watch wasn't working, and the words and cries for help were too late.

The young man's hand came down on top of Charlie. He said *Main Street* in his head, but not from his mouth. It was too late. *Where were the agents?*

Charlie's last memory a hand coming down on top of him and a sharp pain in his neck. A syringe jamming into his carotid artery. Birds gawking... and darkness.

Chapter Thirty-Seven

A low hum banged around the sterile hospital room. The sound of fluorescent lights. Charlie laid on a steel bed. Coldness from the steel chilled his back. His body partially paralyzed. At least, he thought. A sharp pain thumped in the side of his neck. The entry point of the needle.

There was the sound of beeps in the distance. An IV hooked to a machine from his arm. Charlie knew the room. But the room looked altered. *When was I here?* His eyes slowly opened. A person stood above the bed. Nurse Lucy.

An outdated white nurse's outfit and hat greeted Charlie with a smile. "You've had a full week. I didn't think I'd see you here again. I'm Nurse Lucy, you remember me? How are those ribs?"

Charlie didn't speak, and his mouth felt like they were full of marbles. He just stared at the woman with bright lights blazing from behind her head. She was like an angel, but the dark kind. Fuzzy memories swirled in his head from hours ago, weeks, months. *What is real? Why did I know the nurse but had nothing to say?*

"Get some rest. We're going to take good care of you again. You're our chosen one."

Chosen one?

Charlie forced out words. "Where am I?"

"You know, honey. The Boonville Hospital."

"Where are the teens?"

"Teens? What teens?"

"Main Street. Where is Main Street?"

"We're on Main Street. That's where the hospital is. Main Street, Boonville. Just relax, and everything will be fine."

Charlie blinked a couple times. What he wanted to say was not connecting between his brain and mouth. He remembered the chapel and the van. He was alone, and the agents weren't coming. The attack.

What happened? Where are the teens? Are they safe?

Lucy backed away from the steel bed. She grinned. "You have a visitor, son."

The bright lights of the fluorescents shifted like an eclipse as the nurse moved. A unique shape stood above him—a heavy presence. More of the light blocked by the massive figure.

Sheriff John Brown moved into the space and leaned over the bed. He had his right arm in a sling. Something about the sling rang a bell in Charlie's brain. The gunfight at the cemetery.

The sheriff took off his hat and set it aside on a rolling cart next to Charlie's bed. The cart was littered with syringes and other cutting devices. "All we wanted to do was live in peace. Share our message of purpose with the world. We aren't hurting anyone. Then your father and his crew come along and screw everything up. I have the scars to prove it," the sheriff said, holding up his wounded arm in the sling. "But your father understands scars. A different choice years back, and he'd be living his dreams out here in Boonville. Happiness is Our Last Name."

Charlie tried to speak. He felt anger inside for the sheriff despite the words to express the anger not coming to the surface. His brain was garbled.

"I'm not sure what your father has told you. He likes to stretch the truth. Most likely told you terrible things about me and our community. I'd take it with a grain of salt. I wanted to help him find the path of truth, but he resisted. I sacrificed so much for him and got little in return. A student is never above his Master. But your father had this reversed. I've dreamed about this day for many years."

The nurse moved in, crossed her arms, and nodded along.

"We have something special going on here in Boonville. A light on a hill in a world of darkness. We want to expand our message of purpose to the world. And the good news is you'll get to be one of our messengers. Think of it as a second chance. Your father failed all those many years ago. He resisted the path of righteousness. But now's your chance. The second I met you, I knew you were different from your father. What do you say?"

Charlie found a burst of energy somewhere deep inside. His mind cleared for a second, and his words burst out. "Go to hell. You're an evil man, and you've hurt many people. Don't talk about my dad. He has integrity you know nothing about. Where is he? Where are the agents, the teens? The Source is going down."

The sheriff gave a weak smile and then glanced at the nurse.

Charlie reached for the IV sticking out of his right arm and yanked. The nurse yelled out to stop pulling on the tubes. "Please don't do that, son. We have you on specific medications. You're in no shape to leave."

The sheriff gave the nurse a nod. "It's okay, Lucy. He won't get far. This is all normal."

The nurse stepped back from the table.

Charlie sat up in the bed, the lights blinding him. His head was fuzzy. "I'm not staying here. Where's my dad and the rest of our crew?"

The sheriff stared at Charlie. His brown eyes piercing the insides of Charlie. He crossed his arms and gave a smirk. "Don't worry about them now. They won't be in our way."

Charlie flung his feet over the side of the bed. The opposite side of the sheriff. He placed his feet on the floor.

Lucy said, "Be careful. The medicine won't let you get very far."

"Son, I'd listen to Nurse Lucy. There's nowhere to run. And escaping Boonville isn't an option. We have too much work to do."

Charlie placed weight on the balls of his feet. His head spinning and eyes filled with fuzzy lines. "I don't care, I'm leaving. I'll find my way. Do what you have to do."

Charlie gripped the rail of the bed and tried to walk past the sheriff and the nurse. A chilly breeze rushed across his backside because Charlie only wore a paper gown and boxer briefs.

Brown told the nurse to let him go. "He won't get far. We'll clean up the mess later."

Charlie limped into the doorway of the room. He checked right and then left down the hallway. He chose left.

The sheriff called on his walkie talkie to some officers down the hall to watch out for Charlie. The nurse called over the loudspeaker in the hospital. "We have a code red. Please be advised."

Charlie limped down the hallway. He noticed none of the

rooms had patients. Boonville was a small town, but no patients?

He marched down the hallway and passed a nurse's station. Empty computers and chairs and no nurses. He didn't see any other doctors making rounds either. He glanced back down the hall and noticed nurse Lucy and the sheriff standing in the hallway. They were shaking their heads.

Charlie worked hard to keep walking. Each step felt like his feet were in wet cement, about to dry. His eyes flickering in and out of clarity, shifting to black spots. Like a TV set finding a clean signal.

He found another hallway that veered to the right and followed it. He wanted to see a familiar face: Dad, Katie, Sanchez, the agents, anyone. Fear was washing over his body as the hospital a labyrinth with no exit. Pain in his legs and brain, not firing on all cylinders.

Room after room... no patients, no doctors, no nurses, and no sounds. Only the hum of fluorescent lights. The beating of his own heart.

A police officer stood at the end of the hallway in front of an elevator. Charlie was scared to go that direction, but did anyway. Found the idea of someone other than the sheriff and the nurse comforting. Another human, perhaps a good one, most likely not. But he didn't care; he wanted out.

Charlie reached the elevator, and the police officer was stoic. Just nodded his cap and acted like nothing out of the ordinary was happening. He said something about the weather being humid tonight. Charlie thought it strange to need an officer in an empty hospital.

Where were the teens? Dad, Katie, Sanchez, and the agents? Charlie thought as he tapped on the elevator buttons. The doors opened, and the officer tipped his hat and said, have a nice evening. Charlie went down two floors. The doors opened, and he was in the hospital's lobby. An empty lobby.

He felt woozy. The pain in his neck ramped up. Vision blurred. Ankle sore. Charlie wobbled like a zombie down the center of the empty lobby.

He limped to the sliding doors leading out into the parking lot. He stood under the overhang. No cars, no people waiting, no patients coming inside. Only Charlie's beating heart and paper gown blowing in the humid Missouri evening.

Charlie was trying to hold it together. Fear and anxiety built up in his bones. He limped right toward Main Street and found the Boonville Hotel. The paper gown blowing in the wind as he entered. Charlie rushed through the sliding doors. He walked to the massive desk in the lobby. Panic.

A girl that looked a lot like Katie smiled. Only a little older. "Where's Katie?"

"Katie, who? Sorry, no, Katie works here. We have three people working at the desk. No Katie, I'm aware of."

"Stop lying. This entire town is filled with liars. I need to see Katie. She's my girlfriend."

The girl examined the paper gown Charlie was wearing. "Do you need help? I can get you a room for the night? On the house."

"No, I don't want a room. I hate this hotel. I just need to see Katie. Please get her. She'll explain everything."

The night manager shrugged. "Maybe you have her name confused?"

"Stop playing with my head. I know her name. Where are the teens? Where is Jim Tanner?" Charlie said, grabbing his head. A pounding headache growing in his frontal lobe.

"Teens? Jim? Do you want to use a phone?" the girl asked.

Charlie grabbed the corner of the desk. He tried to focus on his weakening legs and his words.

He hung his head.

"I'm not crazy. I just need to talk to my dad."

The room spun on its access. The girl that looked like Katie leaned over the counter, and her lips were moving. No words. No sound.

The words faded to black.

Charlie hit the floor.

Chapter Thirty-Eight

The girl from the hotel knelt down next to Charlie's unconscious body. She tapped his face. Charlie slowly came back to life and shot up. His buns cold on the tile floor because of the open paper gown.

"What happened? I did everything they said. I stayed calm. Sanchez promised we'd be in and out. Clean and fast."

The girl scratched her head, happy that Charlie was alert. "I'm sure you did. Is there someone I can call? This Sanchez guy?"

"No," Charlie said, stumbling to his feet. "I'm done with this place."

Charlie turned and ran out the front door of the Boonville Hotel onto Main Street. The girl raised her hand and yelled something. Charlie only heard a faint voice.

He turned left and ran. No strategy and no particular place to go. Anywhere but Boonville. He ran down Main Street, past the bakery, bank, and law offices. No people, and only an occasional car driving by.

Charlie passed through Main as the city gave way to the country. Open fields and spread out houses. The night fell like a heavy coat on the shoulders of Charlie. A half-moon hung above. Charlie glanced to the glowing ball of light and wished he'd lived on another planet. *Anywhere but Boonville.*

He ran and ran, staying close to the shoulder on the highway. Same highway he'd driven in the Honda. The same highway where the crash happened. The same highway where his life changed forever.

Charlie ran on the same road that took him into Happy town. The town that never lets you go. *Maybe this time it will be different?*

He reflected on the days in Boonville. It was a simple mission to deliver the teens to church camp. They were found, and now they're missing? *Are they okay? What happened at the chapel? Who attacked me?*

Charlie slowed down. He bent over, taking a deep breath and catching his air. The drugs were still strong in his system. He felt woozy, but the adrenaline outpaced the pain. He would not stop until he was home. Until he had answers. Until he found his crew.

He scanned the road with no signs of life. Charlie had no plan, but for a moment, felt safe. Something about the bright light of the moon comforted his aching feet and burning lungs. He thought about Katie, her smile, and the rides in the Honda, and Beach Boy music. *Lying on a beach didn't sound all that bad right now.*

But the moment of safety flipped and was replaced with dread. Nowhere to go, no home, no family. *Run from this God-forsaken place was the only rational thing to do.* The only thing that made sense. A rational thing and a scary one.

Charlie took a deep breath and tried to jog another few

hundred yards. Each burst of running-jogging only wearing him down more.

He hugged the shoulder as to avoid any cars headed in his direction. No cars had passed in the hour or so since leaving Boonville. He ran until his legs gave out. Charlie took a break next to a large road sign. He slumped on the gravel and rested his burning feet and lungs.

He propped himself against the sign. Charlie turned to read the words:

Boonville: Happiness is Our Last Name.

What a load of crap, Charlie thought.

Charlie rose to his feet and kicked the sign stubbing his toe. He yelled out in pain. A mixture of laughter and wanting to cry. A moment of relief for all that had transpired in the week. He realized how ridiculous he must've looked to the girl in the hotel. A paper gown, Adidas sneakers, and no socks. *Loser.*

He stood back from the sign. *A town of plastic smiles. A pseudo happiness that sucks in the searching and innocent only to rip away that same innocence. Offering fake hopes and dreams and purpose.*

He thought about Katie and wondered where she'd gone. *Why didn't the girl in the hotel know her? Was this Sheriff's play? Why did the town feel different despite appearing the same?*

Charlie wanted to rip out the Boonville sign but resisted the urge. He felt a burst of energy. But instead of running, he switched to a walk. He walked and walked and walked. The curve in the highway a familiar scene. He kept walking and dreamed about seeing Kansas City in the distance. Home.

About fifty yards ahead on the side of the road, a van was flipped on its side. Charlie sped up the pace. Letters on the side of the van said:

New Day Community Church

What, New Day? Another crash? Is this a dream? Charlie said, pinching his sweaty skin.

Charlie walked the perimeter of the van. *Not the church van.* He scratched his head.

The first car in hours rumbled along the gravel shoulder. A Ford F-350 truck pulled up next to the van. "Hey, buddy. Name's Roger, friends call me Snake. Can I help? Looks like your van's in rough shape?"

Charlie ran up to the truck. "Snake, I'm so glad to see you. Remember me... Charlie Tanner? The one taking the church group to camp. The crash. You dropped me off at the police department. Remember?"

The tattooed and bald man leaned across the seats and out the passenger window. "I'm sorry, kid. You have me confused with someone else. I was just coming home from a Royals game in Kansas City. I saw the wreck and thought I'd help. But I'd be happy to take you to the police department. They'll take good care of you. Sheriff Brown is the best."

"This isn't my van. Please tell me you're kidding. I rode in your truck. You talked about how great Boonville is. Nothing?"

"Boonville is a special place. But no, I'm sorry, never met you. If that's not your van. Why you out here?"

Charlie waved off the comment. "Long story, doesn't matter. And no. I'm never going back to Happy Land. It's false advertising."

"Suit yourself. Catch you later," Snake said, peeling out back onto the dark highway.

Was it the medicine? Am I going crazy? A dream?

Charlie wanted to cry and scream and explode. For the first time, he wanted to die. Charlie wanted out of the dream or nightmare or universe that no longer made sense. He wanted things back to normal. Charlie wished he'd never taken the kids to camp.

He kept walking. Moon hanging high in the sky, shoving light onto the quiet highway. Charlie followed the gravel bend around the highway, the air warm, and a light breeze.

He walked for another hour. Then it happened again. No closer to Kansas City. No closer to home. Only closer to Boonville.

The Boonville sign, more highway, open spaces, spaced out houses, and then neighborhoods, and Main Street. Legs tired, calves sore, and blisters formed on his heels from the moisture in his sneakers. Paper gown in tatters.

The lights of Main Street placed a pit of nausea in Charlie's stomach. The hotel, police department, and hospital sent angry memories into his mind. A bank, ice cream shop, and law offices, the Missouri River, all part of the nightmare.

The town would not leave Charlie alone. It spit him back into her orbit.

Charlie slumbered down Main Street, no stores open, as it was the middle of the night. No direction, no place to go, no home, only wanting to run.

Charlie found a curb. He sat and cried.

A voice came from behind—a familiar tone.

"The medicine has probably worn off. Give him another dose."

A syringe plunged into the neck of Charlie in the middle of Main Street.

The last words he heard:

We're here to help you. Trust us. Don't listen to the demonic voices of the world. Everything you need is inside our family. You'll be safe. We will be your family. Everything you need is here in Boonville.

Chapter Thirty-Nine

Charlie awoke in a cabin sleeping in a twin bed. A simple room with an end table, chair, and desk in the corner. An attached bathroom. It was similar in dimensions to his room at the Boonville Hotel. He sat up in the comfortable bed and yawned, shaking off his sleep.

Rested and awake. Charlie's body no longer hurt. *How long have I been sleeping? Where am I?*

Charlie glanced down to a plain white tee shirt and black sweatpants. Nothing he owned or ever wore to bed. More of a basketball shorts and tank top guy. He glided to the one window in the room and pushed the plain white curtains aside.

The sun beat through the space, and the warmth a welcomed friend on Charlie's face. He looked out on an expansive grassy field, a smattering of flowers, trees, and wild grasses. He glanced left to rows of cabins. A tree here and there, playground, larger building, and people, lots and lots of people of various ages.

Charlie exited the cabin with a mixture of calm and nerves.

The place new and, at the same time, familiar. He stepped out onto a porch that led down a couple steps. He walked barefoot through the grass and watched kids playing tag in the long grass. Everyone looked happy and not a care in the world.

Charlie enjoyed the grass brushing the soles of his feet. He watched the families playing, eating, and enjoying the day. A man playing a guitar sang a song, and a couple people sat around singing along. A dad tossed his infant in the air and caught him while the child laughed in jubilation.

What is this place? It feels new and the same. Where am I?

Charlie continued to walk through the grass and came upon a girl. She was lying down in the grass and reading a book. She didn't notice Charlie coming up to her. He knelt down.

"Excuse me. Where are we?"

"Paradise," she said, folding the book and glancing up to Charlie.

Charlie stood upright. Taken back by the girl. "Katie? I'm so glad to see you," he said, leaning in for a hug.

She held out a straight arm. "Excuse me? I don't know you. I appreciate the gesture, but I don't hug on first dates. What's your name?"

"Charlie Tanner. Come on, seriously? Is this one of your lame jokes?"

"Sorry, no jokes here."

Charlie was panicking. He saw the seriousness in the eyes of Katie, and she wasn't playing around. "I have a familiar face. What section of The Source compound do you live? Maybe you're confusing me with someone else."

"The Source? This is their compound?"

"Yeah, silly. Only members allowed inside," she said, bending a page in the book to mark her page. She looked up at

Charlie and then tossed the book on the ground, "Oh, my word. I'm so sorry, Master. I didn't recognize you. Such disrespect. Please forgive me. Thank you for everything you're doing for our community."

Charlie spun around in a circle and scanned the grassy field. The voices of laughter and singing echoed through the peaceful compound. He was losing his mind. *Was this a nightmare? Please wake up now, this can't be.*

"Master? What the heck are you saying, Katie? I'm no Master. I'm Charlie Tanner. Your boyfriend from Kansas City. The Beach Boy loving kid that tried to rescue you from this place. I've been to The Source compound, and this ain't it."

Katie fluttered her eyelashes. "I'm flattered. But I'm in a relationship. Why would I ever leave this place? Happiness is Our Last Name. You've taken our community to another level since you've been on the leadership council."

Charlie shouted, "Please, stop saying that. I'm not part of this crazy cult. You're my girlfriend. I lost you. I went to the hotel, and you were gone. Do you work at the Boonville Hotel?"

"Of course not. You're familiar with the laws of The Source. Members can't work jobs outside the community unless for special circumstances or if you're on hiatus. I'd never do that because I love it here."

Charlie pointed at Katie. "Stop it! You were on hiatus when we met. You were going to leave. How can you say you love it here? Please stop the games. What's going on?"

Katie placed the book under her arm. "You're scaring me. I think you should see the medical staff. Please leave me alone. I'm sorry if I offended you."

Katie walked away and picked up the pace with a light jog. She disappeared over a hill and behind a cabin.

Charlie turned around and heard the kids laughing and people singing in the distance. The sounds becoming less calming and more annoying. He didn't know what to do or where to go. *Head back to the cabin? Did I wake up in the middle of a dream?* He pinched himself all over. Nothing.

He picked up the pace and made his way through the grass to a section of buildings. A center square with a store and wild animals in pens around the edge. He rushed into the general store. A man in his mid-thirties read a newspaper behind the counter.

Charlie was not convinced he'd woken up at The Source. He said, "Where are we?"

The man readjusted his eyes. "Oh, man. I didn't know royalty was in here. Hello, Master? What was the question? If it's what I think you said, funny. Thanks for all you're doing for the community."

The man adjusted his hat and revealed his face. "What can I help you with?"

"Sanchez? How are you, man? I just saw Katie, and she didn't recognize me. Is she messing around?"

"Katie? Not sure who that is. Yeah, my name is Rick Sanchez. But..." he paused a beat, "This is the first time we've met. How do you know me? Am I in trouble?"

"What? No. I'm Charlie Tanner. Remember, the operation at the chapel? You worked with my dad, Jim. Are you and Katie in on this?"

He laughed. "No, sorry, man. No recollection of a Katie or Jim. But that sounds like a good prank."

"Where are the teens? Are they okay?"

"What teens? There are some teens hanging out in section three. Again, let me plead the fifth. But thanks for all you're doing for the community. We've grown a ton from your leadership."

Charlie stopped listening. He turned in defeat and limped out of the store. He pushed the screen door open and stood at the front of the store, examining the massive landscape of The Source compound.

It was ten times larger than the one before. It had many of the same buildings, but dozens more. Same layout, but hundreds of more acres.

Charlie wanted to cry. He wanted to die. The good night's sleep and rested body were now replaced with worry and anxiety. *How am I on the leadership council? Where is my dad and the sheriff?*

Charlie found a picnic bench under a tree. He slumped onto the hardwood. He watched people pass by—old, young, black, white, and everything in between.

A young girl stopped at the table. She was about eighteen. "Thanks for everything, Master Tanner."

Charlie smiled and thanked the girl with hesitation. He took a second look at her face. She was a girl in his youth group. "Hey, aren't you, Greta Harvey?"

She nodded. "Outstanding work. How'd you know my name?"

"Are you from Kansas City?"

"Nope. I'm from Boonville. Happiness is Our Last Name," she said, in a robotic tone.

Charlie rose from the table. "No, you're Great Harvey from Kansas City. And your folks go to my dad's church. You sit in the front right chairs every Sunday. I took you to church camp, and we got in an accident. What happened? Why are you here? Have they brainwashed you?"

"Sorry, Master. You're mistaken. I've lived my entire life here. I gotta go..." she said, skipping away.

Charlie slammed his hand on the table. He rubbed his temples and felt like his brain was on the brink of explosion.

A voice came from behind the table—a whisper.

We're here to help you. Trust us. Don't listen to the demonic voices of the world. Everything you need is inside our family. You'll be safe. We will be your family. Everything you need is here in Boonville.

Chapter Forty

Sheriff John Brown found a seat at the table. He removed his gun and placed it on the table. "We've been waiting for this moment for a long time. I'm sure you have more questions than answers. But things will make sense in due time. The important thing is you're safe, and you're here. The Happiest Town on earth."

Charlie observed the words coming out of the sheriff's mouth. He was lost in their trance. Everything Brown said was mostly lies, but this time was different. Charlie just let him talk and had no conception of the blurred lines between lies and truth.

Brown said, "You've done amazing work in a short time. Not surprising as you are the chosen one."

Charlie gave into the weirdness. The *chosen one* talk. He calmly sat at the table and gave into the craziness that is Sheriff John Brown and The Source. "I'm not sure what's going on. I don't even pretend this is all normal. I've given up on finding a rational explanation for this place. But I have one question."

Brown folded his hands. "Anything, Charlie. What's nagging you?"

"Did you cause the crash?"

Brown unfolded his hands, leaned back on the bench, and sighed. "Not my proudest moment. But it had to be done. None of this would've happened," he said, turning and taking in the compound's landscape.

"Did you not consider that we might've died? Wasn't this all about getting back at my father for standing up to you, anyway?"

"Our relationship is complicated. Water under the bridge. We were young. Did things out of youthful angst. Let's not live in the past. What matters is the future of The Source and Boonville. And you're going to lead us into the promised land."

"Youthful angst involves murder? Did you kill my dad too? Where is he?"

Brown smiled and twirled the gun sitting on the table. "He's around here somewhere. So is your entire family. A big happy family, those Tanner's. Not my idea, but we make it work."

"Wait, what? My folks are here? They live here and not Kansas City?"

"Yeah, for the last couple of years. Since you came onto the leadership council."

Charlie took a few deep breaths and worked to not lose his cool. "Not possible. My dad has worked for years to take you down. No way they live here. Did you brainwash them? Is that why Katie and Sanchez have no clue who I am? Call me Master. Whatever that means?"

Brown gave a belly laugh. "We don't use the term *brain-washing*. More sophisticated of a process. The same process we used on the teens. I'll hand it to you. Jim and the agents were oh so close from discovering our little secret. Just a little slow.

The raid on the chapel would've worked if not for our own intelligence. 'We're always watching you.' Let's say they all got a taste of our S-Meter."

"Seriously? That pseudo-science crap doesn't work. It's a placebo. It's a Scientology rip off which used the same ideas with no results."

Brown folded his hands again. He was amused with the intensity of Charlie. Another reason he'd be a perfect leader for the next generation. "No problem, you walk by faith, I'll walk by sight. Explain why Katie, Sanchez, and the teens don't know who you are? Remember the kid you met on Main Street when you tried to escape? How come that teen didn't remember you, either? Still a placebo? Pseudo-science?"

"Yeah, and you want me to believe Boonville just spits people back when they try to leave? What kind of voodoo is that?"

"Charlie... we can't share all our secrets."

Charlie rose from the table. He wasn't satisfied with the answers of the sheriff. "Regardless of your methods of madness, it's still madness. Brainwashing is brainwashing. Are you saying these devices erase the memories of our pasts? You think that's ethical? How can you justify erasing the essence of these people? If we don't have memories, good or bad, we have nothing. It makes us into the people we are."

"Who says people aren't already brainwashed? G. K. Chesterton said, 'When men stop believing in God, they don't believe in nothing. They believe in anything.' Let's say we help the process along. We want people to believe in Truth, not any old buffet of ideas. We think our way is the best. Of course, I'm biased. What's the harm in this?"

"The problem is you're messing with the core of people. You don't have the right. People need to find their way on their own. Nobody denies the world is full of lies and distortions.

But who's saying what you teach is the truth? Who says what you're preaching isn't ruining people's lives? I recall your teachings leading to some violent acts. Agent Sanchez and Lindsey Sparks ring a bell? The girl you murdered when you mentored my dad?"

The sheriff nodded. "Yes, you're right, Charlie. We've all done bad things. Things we regret. But what if we could erase those mistakes? What if we could undo all the bad we've ever done like it never happened? Replace the painful parts of our pasts with new futures? Imagine the kind of world we could build? That's the world I want to build together."

Charlie hung his head. A mess of emotions and swirling with contradictory ideas. *Why am I entertaining the ideas of this mad man? I know who this guy is. He's rotten at the core.*

"How do you bring back Lindsey Sparks and Melissa Morris? Did you erase those parts of your brain?"

The sheriff smiled and held up a finger. He then mumbled something into his walkie-talkie strapped to his shoulder.

A young girl and an older woman appeared from behind the tree near the picnic table. "What if we fine-tuned these so-called placebos, pseudo-science devices, into one of the most powerful tools in the universe? Not only erasing the pain and memories of the past. But could also bring people back from the dead?" Brown said.

The older woman had greying streaks in her blonde hair and a youthful charm. She stood next to Brown and said, "Hello, I'm Melissa Morris. I used to be friends with your dad."

The younger woman standing next to the older woman had dark hair and was about twenty. She said, "Hello, I'm Lindsey Sparks. Good to see you again, Charlie."

Charlie stood in silence. He waited for a hidden camera crew to come out and say this was all a reality TV show. He waited for his mother to wake him from his bed in Kansas City.

A late-night after watching a show downtown caused Charlie to have nightmares. *That's all this was. Rational explanation.*

Charlie, for a second, remembered the day he took the church van keys from his dad. The waving parents and laughing and farting in the van. *Was it last week or five years ago, who knew?* But Charlie wished he'd stepped up to his dad and said no. Leaned into his own future, not the one-handed down from well-intentioned parents.

He wanted to find himself on his own terms. Ministry and counseling wasn't the path for Charlie despite making his father happy. Another Tanner in a long line of clergyman. Charlie wanted none of it.

But in the span of time during the chaos of Boonville, he wondered something that felt inauthentic. It came from contradictory places in the soul. It made little sense after going through the hell of the Happy Town. Not possible.

For a moment, at the compound of The Source, standing next to a madman and two ladies that apparently rose from the dead, Charlie wondered if a place like Boonville *was everything he'd ever wanted. Were the voices true?*

Amid the plastic smiles and the pace of country living foreign to an urban kid from Kansas City. With his family nearby, Katie around despite not knowing the Charlie of the past, Sanchez, and the teens finding a second chance in Boonville. A built-in family with a body of weird teachings and technology he wasn't comfortable with. A sheriff from the depths of hell. And a calling to lead the next generation as the chosen one.

Charlie had a thought, many thoughts, that made little sense to an outside observer. But thoughts nonetheless forced upon Charlie because he was alone. He had no other options. He had to deal with reality. A reality that blurred the lines of fantasy, fiction, truth, and lies.

His reality in front of him now, today, here.

Was The Source the place I was meant to find all along? Was this the path of my searching? The safe and secure place we all dream and pray about?

Charlie watched the women stare back at him with smiles and giggles. The sheriff puffing out his chest with the pride of accomplishing what no one has ever done, except one: conquer death.

Was I giving in? Was I too judgmental with The Source from the beginning? Not everything in the church rides the rails of truth and strays into the weeds of destruction.

Maybe The Source had something to teach me?

Charlie was an outsider. He hadn't drunk the Kool-Aid like the others, from what he could tell. But this outsider now had moved to an insider on the leadership council. A team committed to spreading a message of purpose and freedom.

Spider-Man said with great power comes great responsibility. Charlie now had a lifetime of responsibility to figure out how to use this new power for good and not evil. Could Charlie guide The Source into a new future? Time will tell.

Epilogue

Charlie Tanner awoke in his bedroom. A bedroom much like the one in his suburban Kansas City home. Beach Boys pictures on the walls. Guitar in the corner. Record player on the other side with a stack of albums. Mostly Classic Rock. Kansas City Chiefs Super Bowl poster framed above the bed.

He slipped out of bed, feet on the floor, took a deep breath. The days before were a blur. He pulled back the curtain across the only window in the space. The tree-lined streets were picturesque. Colors of reds and yellows suggested fall in Missouri. The neighborhood, much like the suburban Kansas City area Charlie spent his entire life.

Families sat in the yard and played with their kids and pets. Many of the homes designs were similar, with only slightly different color schemes. An older couple swung on a porch swing, sipping on mugs of their favorite drinks.

Charlie scanned the yard and then his watch. It was almost noon. *What is this place?* The home and neighborhood felt like the house in Kansas City, but different. Similar street but not the same neighbors.

He stumbled down the stairs, scratching his bedhead. The foyer opened into a large dining room with a long table, chairs, and fine china in a cabinet against the wall. The smells of eggs and bacon came from the kitchen off the dining room.

Charlie's mother June opened a swinging door from the kitchen wearing an apron and carrying a plate of food. She gave a wide smile. "Sleep good? You had a big week."

"I think so," Charlie said, scratching his groin. "Where are we?"

Jim came into the dining room from a study on the opposite end of the house. "You've always had a great sense of humor. Good to see you, kid. I'm so glad everything went smoothly at camp. I knew you could do it."

Charlie glanced at June and then Jim. "What are you talking about?"

Jim gave a soft punch on Charlie's arm. "Church camp, funny guy. The parents said their kids had a great time. Thanks for driving them."

"Dad, have you lost your mind? The kids are missing. We had a crash, and the van flipped. I called and called, and you never answered. They trapped me in Boonville."

June placed the plate of eggs and bacon on the dining room table. She wiped her hands on the apron and then hugged Charlie. "That sounds like one of your short stories. Are you working on new material? You get silly when you're hungry. Eat up. You must be exhausted," she said, sliding the plate in front of a high-back chair, "Come on, eat. You're skin and bones."

"Mom... Dad... I'm not hungry. This isn't fiction. Everything went bad in Boonville. The teens are missing, and I almost got killed in Boonville."

Jim gently wrapped his muscular arms around Charlie. "Ok, the comedy routine is over. We *live* in Boonville, son. You took the kids to a camp in Arkansas. I talked to the parents yesterday. The kids had a blast. Have some eggs, take a shower, and you can get back to work."

"Am I still working as a pastoral assistant at the church?"

Jim crossed his arms. "Funny, kid. Not sure where you got that information. You did a favor for Sheriff Brown taking the kids to camp. Your job is much more important. You're leading The Source with the leadership council."

Everything was a test. Charlie couldn't explain the house. *Why did the street look like Kansas City, but different?* Charlie was testing the memory of his parents. *Was this all a dream? Did they have their memories wiped by The Source?* All indicators pointed to yes.

Charlie looked at their faces. Faces that were the same and different. Dad had a few more wrinkles, and his mother's blonde hair had more gray. They appeared five years older. *How would I know?*

"What is wrong with your guys? Did you get older when I was gone?"

June said, "We're all getting older, Charlie. Not sure what you mean. You were only gone a week. Do I look that bad?" June said, flipping her hair.

"Enough with the old people jokes. Eat up and then get to work. You have a lot of responsibility in this town."

The test worked. Only confirming in Charlie's mind what the sheriff said was true. But why the house? Where are the cabins? The compound was different and more expansive.

A young man about two years younger than Charlie came down the stairs. It was his brother Owen. "Hey, Master. Don't you have more important things to do than kiss up to Mom and Dad?"

Charlie stood silent, like seeing a ghost.

"I'm going to get some fresh air," Charlie said, rushing out the front door.

He found a wooden rocker on the porch and settled down. The neighborhood felt heavy and strange. The comfort of the family no longer a comfort. A nuisance. More complexity and stories to navigate. Faces the same yet aged, but not the people he left however long he'd been gone.

Charlie gently rocked in the chair. He watched the happy people in the Happy Town do happy things. *But was it real? Did they know what lurked beneath the city streets and the lies behind The Source? Were their minds wiped clean?* Would Charlie be able to convince others not to be fooled by the plastic smiles in this plastic town?

Charlie watched a police cruiser slowly drive down the street. The man inside glanced side to side, scanning the streets. Charlie thought *that must be a boring job in this town.*

Sheriff John Brown stopped the car in front of Charlie's house. He rolled down the window, gave a wave, and tipped his hat.

He smiled and drove off.

Charlie then remembered not to be fooled by the facade of Boonville. This town was anything but Happy.

A Note at the End

Boonville was a National Novel Writing Month novel (nanowrimo.org). A writing competition where hundreds of thousands of brave souls attempt to write a 50,000 word rough draft of a novel in 30 days. It's a blast to participate and a great motivator for a prolific writer like myself. I've competed in the event for the last eight years.

Every year, when November comes around, I'm searching for ideas. In the summer of 2020, I visited Boonville. A real place about 90 minutes outside Kansas City, Missouri. It's a historic town near the Missouri River and a great place to visit. Lots of outdoor adventures, art, shops, and room to breathe. I'm a city-guy, and any chance to explore smaller cities and towns a welcomed friend.

So as I wandered the streets of Main Street in Boonville, a story idea emerged. I asked the typical What If Questions...

What if a cult was operating in a small town? What if that said cult was evil and pretended to be good for the town? What if someone drove to Boonville and couldn't leave?

And on it went until I had a seed of an idea. An idea that stuck around until November when I started NANOWRIMO.

I've always loved books like Wayward Pines and shows like Twin Peaks and Stranger Things, which portray small towns with mysterious things and people rumbling behind the scenes. Towns that appear serene and calm and yet are filled with mayhem and evil. A place like my version of Boonville.

Boonville was a blast to write, and I hope it gave you a couple hours of fun. I'm working on Book 2 and 3 for a trilogy. Don't relax, because Book 2 is going to get crazy and take Charlie, Katie, and the Sheriff into unexpected places. Hope to have that out later in the year.

Thanks for your support!

Ryan J. Pelton

January 2021

Help Me Reach More Readers

ENJOY THIS BOOK? YOU CAN MAKE A BIG DIFFERENCE!

If you loved this book, you can help me reach more readers with a few easy steps:

(1) Review This Book

Reviews are one of the best helps for getting these stories out to the world. My publisher doesn't have the financial muscle of New York, but does have an even more potent weapon. A bunch of loyal and committed readers. By leaving an honest review other readers can find and take chances on my books. Just go to the site you purchased this book, search for the title, and leave a review. Much thanks in advance!

(2) Subscribe To My Email List

Building a relationship with my readers is the greatest joy of my writing life. I'm not just a writer, and love sharing things I'm learning, reading, and pondering. If you want an occasional update on the latest novels, novellas, short stories, and my other writing projects. If you'd like to hear about things in my world, get some interesting links, and book updates please do so below. I also give special deals and other cool insider goodies to my VIP List. Sign up today, and join the fun! ryanjpeltonbooks.com

(3) Tell Your Friends

Word of mouth is still the best marketing there is, so I would love if you gave a shout out to your family and friends about this book, and the others I have written. You can find a comprehensive list of my fiction books at: attentionbooks.com

Thanks again for your help, and thanks for reading!

About the Author

Ryan J. Pelton is a writer, speaker, coach, and ordained pastor, passionate about storytelling. With over 23 published books spanning a variety of genres, Ryan embraces the title of Genre-Nomad.

He is also the founder of Attention Books, an independent publisher dedicated to amplifying unique voices, and the host of The Art of Paying Attention podcast, where Ryan interviews world-class artists, writers, entrepreneurs, leaders, and creatives.

When he's not writing, you can find Ryan spending time with his family, reading an eclectic mix of books, or contemplating life over a taco.

Connect with Ryan and stay updated on new releases, articles, and exclusive content:

📖 Website: ryanjpeltonbooks.com or attentionbooks.com

📷 Instagram: @ryanjpelton

📫 Newsletter: attentionbooks.com/subscribe

Also by Ryan J. Pelton

Fiction

Dexter O'Kane Series

Hired Gun (Book 1)

Stranger Danger (Book 2)

Color Blood (Book 3)

First Blood (Book 4)

L.A. Dreams (Book 5)

Dexter O'Kane Box Set (Books 1-4)

Stand Alone Titles

The Boardwalk

Corey Island (*novella*)

Watched (*novella*)

Young Adult

Running Down a Dream

Boonville (*Boonville Series Book 1*)

Middle Grade

Ricky Rayburn Series

Secrets of the Ambassadors (Book 1)

Mysterious Pirates of the Pacific (Book 2)

Non Fiction

The Modern Saints

Gospel Driven Leadership

The Gospel Marinated Soul

The Gospel Marinated Life

By Way of Reminder

Gospel Centered Productivity

Everyday Evangelism

40 Days with Jesus

www.ingramcontent.com/pod-product-compliance
Lightning Source LLC
LaVergne TN
LVHW091135080826
845145LV00008B/2159

* 9 7 8 1 9 4 9 4 2 0 1 4 2 *